# The Earth and Sky of Jacques Dorme

*Andreï Makine*

# The Earth and Sky
# of Jacques Dorme

Translated by Geoffrey Strachan

SCEPTRE

Copyright © 2003 Mercure de France
Translation © 2005 Geoffrey Strachan

Originally published in 2003 as *La terre et le ciel de Jacques Dorme*
by Mercure de France, 26 rue de Condé, 75006 Paris, France
This English translation first published in Great Britain in 2005
by Hodder and Stoughton
A division of Hodder Headline

The right of Andreï Makine to be identified as the Author
of the Work has been asserted by him in accordance with
the Copyright, Designs and Patents Act 1988

A Sceptre Book

1 3 5 7 9 10 8 6 4 2

A CIP catalogue record for this title is available from the British Library

ISBN 0 340 83125 1

Typeset in Sabon by Hewer Text Ltd, Edinburgh
Printed and bound by Mackays of Chatham plc, Chatham, Kent

Hodder Headline's policy is to use papers that are natural,
renewable and recyclable products and made from wood grown in
sustainable forests. The logging and manufacturing processes are expected
to conform to the environmental regulations of the country of origin

Hodder and Stoughton Ltd
A division of Hodder Headline
338 Euston Road
London NW1 3BH

# Translator's Note

Andreï Makine was born and brought up in Russia but *The Earth and Sky of Jacques Dorme*, like his other novels, was written in French. The book is set in Russia and France and the author uses some Russian words in the French text which I have kept in this English translation. These include *shapka* (a fur hat or cap, often with earflaps); *izba* (a traditional wooden house built of logs); and *taiga* (the virgin pine forest that spreads across Siberia south of the tundra).

The text contains a number of references to Russian historical figures, including Grigori Aleksandrovich Potemkin, Catherine the Great's administrator for newly-acquired lands in the south, who reputedly gave orders for sham villages to be built for her tour in 1787, and Mikhail Harionovich Kutuzov, Commander-in-Chief of the Russian forces at Borodino in 1812. There are also a number of references to institutions from the Communist era in Russia. A *kolkhoz* was a collective farm. The Pioneers were junior members of the Young Communist youth movement. The GPU (later OGPU) was the agency for investigating and combating counter-revolutionary activities in the USSR from 1922 to 1934. The NKVD, the People's Commissariat for Internal Affairs, were the police charged with maintaining political control during the years of Stalin's purges from 1934 to 1946.

References to French history include allusion to the new calendar established in the early years of the French Revolution, starting with Year I in 1793. Ventôse, one of the newly-named months, corresponded to late February and early March. Year II was one of many political executions, as the Terror continued.

I am indebted to a number of people and, in particular, the author, for their advice, assistance and encouragement in the preparation of this translation. To all of them my thanks are due, notably Amber Burlinson, Ludmilla Checkley, Bruce Crisp, June Elks, Geoffrey Ellis, Alison Fell, Scott Grant, Don Hill, Russell Ingham, Pierre Sciama, Claire Squires, Simon Strachan, Susan Strachan and, above all, my editor at Sceptre, Carole Welch.

G.S.

for Carole and Laurent

# One

The span of their life together is to be so short that everything will happen to them for both the first and last time.

Amid the fierceness of their lovemaking early in the night he snapped the thread of the old necklace she never took off. The little amber beads clattered onto the floor and as the rain began to fall, it at first mimicked this fine rattle of grapeshot, then changed its tune, turning into a downpour, torrents of water and, ultimately, an ocean surge that flooded into the room. After a blazing hot day, with the dry wind rustling like insect wings, this tidal wave reaches their naked bodies, filling the sheets with the damp aroma of leaves, the bitter freshness of the plains. The wall facing the bed does not exist, only gaps in the charred timbers, the havoc wrought by the fire of two weeks ago. Beyond this space the purple, resinous flesh of the stormy sky swells heavily. The first and last May storm of their shared life.

She gets up, draws the table towards the corner most sheltered from the deluge, then pauses beside the shattered wall. He stands, goes to join her, slips his arms about her, his mouth buried in her hair, his gaze lost in the seething darkness outside the breach. A long, wringing wet tissue of wind clings to their skin; the man shivers and murmurs in the woman's ear: 'So you never feel the cold, then . . .' She laughs softly: 'I've been out here on the steppes for over twenty years. And you . . . A year? There you are . . . You'll get used to it. You'll see . . .'

A train shakes the track heavily, very close to the house. The puffing of the engine cuts into the darkness, through the rain. The mass of coaches comes to a halt beneath the windows, the beam from a lamp rakes through the room. The man and woman are silent, pressed close together. From the train there arises a blend of sibilant voices, groans, a long gasp of pain. Men wounded beyond repair for the front, being evacuated into the depths of the country. It is strange to feel his own body so alive and still stirred by pleasure. This woman's shoulders held in his fingers' caress, the slow, warm throb of the blood, there in the hollow of his groin. The slithering of an amber bead beneath his foot. And the thought that tomorrow they will have to gather them all up, repair the necklace . . .

Most amazing of all is the very idea of tomorrow, of hunting for those tiny spheres . . . Here, in a house barely seventy miles from the front line, in this country foreign to the woman and still more foreign to the man . . . The train moves off below the windows, begins its rhythmic drumming on the steel. They listen as the jolting sounds fade beneath the swish of the rain. The woman's body is burning hot. 'Out here on the steppes for over twenty years . . .' the man recalls, and smiles in the darkness. Since they met, the day before yesterday, he has had time to talk to her about what has happened in France during those twenty years. As if it were possible to remember everything, as if he could reel off all the events one after the other, starting in 1921, right up to June 1940, when he left the country . . .

The rain bounces off the floor, they feel a veil of dampness over their faces. 'Do you think he'll really be able to get them to accept him?' she murmurs. 'Without an army, without money. It's all very well his being a general . . .' He does not reply at once, struck by the strangeness of these moments: a woman who for so many years had not heard herself called by her true Christian name (what they call her here when speaking to her is 'Shura'; 'Shura' or sometimes 'Alexandra'); himself having become a Russian pilot; this house gutted by an explosion; this township on the banks of a great river, in the middle of the steppes, where preparations are under way for a gigantic battle . . .

A bird frightened by the storm hurtles into the room, weaves a jerky flight through the darkness, makes its escape through the gap.

'It's true he has very few people around him,' murmurs the man. 'And, as for the English, I don't know if we can count on them . . . But you know, it's like a battle in the air. It's not always the number of planes that decides it, nor even how good they are. It's . . . How to explain? It's the air. Yes, the air. Sometimes you feel the air is supporting you, playing on your side. The air or heaven itself. You just have to have great faith in it. For him, too, it's heaven that will play a greater part in this than anything else . . . That's what he believes.'

In the course of this journey I have repeatedly added up the years that separated me from those two lovers.

'Fifty years, give or take a month or two . . .' I tell myself once more, as I observe the monotonous passing of the hours of night over Siberia outside the aircraft's window. Fifty years . . . The number ought to impress me. But instead of amazement I have a vivid sense of the presence of those two beings within me, of their deep connection to what I am.

Outside one can only walk by thrusting a pike or a ski pole into the carapace of snow swept clean by the blizzard. Indoors, in the *izba*'s long dining-room, the steel stove is red hot. The air smells of burning bark, dark-brown tobacco and ninety-degrees-proof spirit laced with cranberry syrup. It is scarcely an hour since I arrived, the goal has been reached, I am there in the house that is known as 'the Edge'. ('It's right at the edge,' a local inhabitant told me, as he showed me the way. 'At the edge of what?' 'Just at the Edge. That's what they call it. It's the last house. You'll see. There's a helicopter pad over there. Mind you, in this blizzard you won't see a thing now. Whatever you do don't let go of the cable!') I began walking, bent double under the snow squalls, my knapsack swaying about on my back, one hand gripping an old ski pole, the other sliding along a thick rope stretched between one house and the next.

Now, in the warmth of this mess room, there is nothing more for me to do but wait for the pitching and tossing the journey has imprinted in my body to calm down. Several days on the train, then the aircraft, finally the terrible tracked vehicle that brought me here across the icy wastes. And the last stage: the interminable hike along that cable swathed in hoar-frost, stumbling painfully to arrive at the Edge. At the edge of what? At the edge of everything. Of inhabited land, of the Arctic, of the polar night. The rope ended there, nailed to the timbers of the very last house.

I manage to move my feet within my boots. My hands, my finger joints are coming back to life, obeying me, I can grip the cup without spilling it, as happened just now. 'The goal has been reached,' I reflect with a smile. I am here in the territory Jacques Dorme once flew over. Tomorrow I shall see the place where a life that I have borne within me since childhood came to grief. His life and that of the woman who had loved him. In the blissful drowsiness of my exhaustion those lives lived long ago come awake beneath my eyelids, revive that tale of a day, a city, the imagined memory of a night. That night when the rain mimicked the staccato rattle of the amber beads . . .

'Tell me, my friend, have you heard the one about the young man from Moscow, a bit like you, who arrives in the *taiga* of Yakutia? Listen. I'll tell you . . .'

One of my hosts is speaking. There are three of them altogether in the house on the Edge. Two are these geologists, both of whom, as they shook hands with me, by a comic coincidence proffered the same name: Lev. Two Leos, two lions, I said to myself, suppressing a smile. The first of them, tall, with broad shoulders, evidently read my mind and sought to clarify matters. 'Now see here. I'm the real lion. He's only a cub . . .' The other, short, and with a face marked by chilblains, exclaimed: 'Shut your mouth, Trotsky!' By way of a welcome I had joined them in a glass of that inhuman brew, alcohol barely sweetened with cranberry juice, and then, with almost magical ease, succeeded in getting myself accepted to join their next day's expedition. 'But of course, my friend. All we have to do is say the word to the pilot and it's as good as done. While we're blowing the mountain to smithereens he'll take you wherever you like.' I took a bottle of brandy I had brought from Paris out of my knapsack and we poured it into three hefty glass tumblers. They drank, exchanged doubtful glances. Russian custom forbids the criticism of fare which is a gift. 'It's . . . good,' Big Lev concluded. 'Yes, not bad,' Little Lev agreed. 'It's like the wine they give you in church. I expect women like it. Do you fancy a drop, Valya?'

Valya, the cook, shook her head in refusal. Her arms white with flour up to the elbows, she was kneading dough on a big table at the other end of the room. An enormous woman: a heavy, rounded bosom thrusting out beneath her thick sweater, a broad backside which, when she sat on a stool, covered the seat completely. Her eyes slanted like those of the Yakut, but her skin very white. A carnal robustness reminiscent of the women of the Ukraine. 'What man could take on such a giantess?' I thought with a mixture of fear and admiration.

8

Now I listen to Little Lev telling this story he has embarked on.

'. . . So there you are. He lands in the middle of the *taiga* all the way from Moscow. He knows nothing, but he's a bit like all of you, keen as mustard. And, straight off, the old Siberians say to him, "If you want to be one of us there are three things you have to do: first, down a bottle of vodka in one; second, screw a Yakut woman; and third, go out into the *taiga* and shake a bear by the paw." Well, your man jumps up, grabs a bottle and, hey presto, downs it in one! Then he runs out into the *taiga*. An hour later he comes back, all covered in scratches, and yells at the top of his voice: "Right. Now show me a Yakut woman and I'll shake her by the paw." Ha, ha, ha . . .'

They choke with laughter, as I do too, infected by their mirth and above all because of the comic pantomime Little Lev starts acting out: the young novice knocking back a pint of spirit, running into the *taiga* and raping a bear. At this moment Valya approaches, bearing a dish of steaming potatoes. Little Lev, still in the middle of his performance, rushes up to her, grapples her from behind, his hands clinging to the woman's hips, his chin digging into her broad back. A female bear assaulted by the Muscovite simpleton. She turns with a smile on her lips but her eyes ablaze with fire: how dare he, this midget? Her hand fetches a blow to Lev's head, just the way a bear's paw would, with nonchalant power. The man is hurled against the wall, his face smeared with flour.

That night the howling of the blizzard forms the single background to all the other noises: the snoring of the two Levs, the crackle of wood in the stove and from time to

9

time the rustle of a page. In the other room Valya is reading the thick book I noticed on a windowsill when I arrived. One of those novels of the sixties where love took its course against a background of vast electricity generating stations under construction, the conquest of the *taiga*, the glorious exploits of the mother country. A fiction actually not too far removed from this woman's life or her dreams? Who knows? I do not notice the moment when she turns out the light.

Towards the middle of the night the lashing of the squalls obliterates anything else the ear might still have heard. I think about the tiny dot of my presence in this corner of the world. What point of orientation can one find? The icy fringe of the Arctic Ocean? The Bering Strait? The Victory Peak, nine thousand feet high, to the west of this house?

I tell myself that, when it comes down to it, nothing places this terrain for me better than the memory of Jacques Dorme's life.

Jacques Dorme's story had kept me company all along my route. The intensity of it turned any given town I was passing through, any railway station, into a blur; it isolated me in the midst of crowds. From Paris I travelled to Warsaw, without difficulty reached the Ukraine (which had recently proclaimed its independence), was then held up for several hours at the totally new frontier with Russia. When pronounced in front of a little hut darkly stained with damp snow, the words 'frontier' and 'visa' sounded straight out of a satirical story by Chekhov. As did the uniforms of the frontier guards, which were of a strangely effeminate cut, likewise the eagles on their *shapkas*, cheap gold braid reminiscent of Christmas tree decorations. And, even more so, the document I offered them. This stateless person's passport, authorising me to visit 'any country except the USSR'. The USSR no longer existed and this prohibition had now taken on a disturbing, almost metaphysical, meaning. Poorly covered in plastic by an old Algerian in the Boulevard Barbès, the document had suffered from the damp and the thin buckled cardboard, with its blurred stamps, was bound to provoke suspicion. Taking pity on my innocence, a lorry driver finally explained to me the measure of alcohol required to cross the frontier. I had with me two bottles of brandy. In his view one of these should suffice. A flat bottle, which the boss of the frontier station slipped into his greatcoat pocket before breathing onto a little indigo ink pad.

It was the first time I had gone back to Russia and I was returning in secret. However, the strangeness of my arrival was soon eclipsed by the bizarre nature, now comic, now painful, of the new state of things. The monument in a Ukrainian town: two figures shaking hands and the legend in letters of gold: 'Long live the Union of the Ukraine with . . .' The rest of it ('. . . Russia') had been torn off. My 'visa', paid for with a bottle of brandy. Then, one evening in Moscow, a gathering of men at the back of an ugly restaurant building. They were shuffling about in the muddy snow of early March, grinning and winking at one another, but their grins were tense, their gaze was fixed on two large windows, open on the ground floor. Inside, in the halo of fluorescent light, a white tiled wall, two mirrors and a hand drier buzzing in the void could be seen. A woman appeared in front of one of the mirrors, unbuttoned her coat and, unconcerned by the presence of the spectators, exposed the naked white-ness of her body. She even spun lightly round on her high heels, revealing very full breasts with brown nipples, the well-rounded triangle of her belly. Another hitched her foot up onto the sill and began tugging at the fastening of her boot. Beneath her miniskirt her leg was exposed right up to the hip, a broad thigh enclosed in red tights . . . This parade, improvised by prostitutes in the toilet area of a restaurant, bore witness to an undeniable liberalization. Less hypocrisy than before, more imagination. 'Progress . . .' I reflected, as I continued on my way.

I was to echo this thought two days later in a large city on the Volga. To kill time while waiting for my train, I let myself be carried along by the crowd and found myself in a park. Amid gaudily painted booths, noisy festivities were under way – some kind of 'town celebration' or, quite simply, a fine Sunday, the previous night's snowfall reflecting the dazzling sunlight. I walked along, stumbling over deep drifts, intoxicated by the sharp freshness of the snows, bonding with the laughter, the glances, the language I no longer needed to translate. This home-coming was like a dream where everything is instantly comprehensible, where physical contact, all hearts beating as one, is wonderfully palpable. Drunk with the sunshine and the gaiety around me, I even had this exalted and sanctimoniously patriotic thought: 'They may only have three roubles in their pockets but here they are, laughing and celebrating in just the way they always did. A country in desperate straits, but what a gift for happiness! Whereas in the West, they would have . . .' My wits dulled by the merriment, I was about to pursue this analytical comparison of mine between the Slavic soul and the soulless West, when suddenly the happiness found its perfect expression, concentrated in the face of a child. A little girl of nine or ten, almost preternaturally beautiful, walking along holding a wo-man's hand – her grandmother's, no doubt. They stopped a few yards away from me, the child looked at me inquiringly. I smiled at her. And suddenly I realized that this incredibly beautiful little face was made up. Discreetly, and by an expert hand, an adult's. Not daubed with a carnival mask but transformed into the thrillingly angelic face of a doll-woman. I also noticed that dusk was beginning to fall, that the booths had closed. My head was still ringing with laughter and sunlight . . . The first streetlamps were flickering with mauve light. The woman turned and stared at me with an appraising eye. Then, fondling the child's chin, murmured: 'The fair's over. You won't get your sweeties now . . .' The child looked hard at me. At the last moment I bit back the words that were on the tip of my tongue: 'You have a very pretty granddaughter . . .' I thought I had guessed what was afoot. The woman tugged at the child's hand and I saw them making their way towards a great prefabricated shed, the 'beer bar'. In a hissed conversation behind my back two market women were heaving outraged sighs: 'Did you see that? The old woman's back again with the kid.' 'Well, what do you expect? That child's her meal ticket . . .' 'I'd hang them, the bastards who do that . . .'

I saw their two figures at the end of the alleyway, the big one and the little one, silhouetted against the lights of the 'beer bar'. I should have caught up with them. Given them all the money I had. Warned the police. Carried off the child . . . But was what I thought I had grasped really going on? All along the alleyway the shutters of the booths were already closed, rays of light filtered out from inside. One could sense the silent presence of the stallholders. The fairground in darkness, these little wooden huts, each with its own secret, the child in her make-up, who had just smiled at me . . . I preferred to believe it was a misunderstanding . . .

The only places where I truly felt at home once more were the corridors of the Metro and the pedestrian subways, now transformed into bazaars of poverty. Old men offered objects for sale that reeked of having been torn out of flats or rooms where their absence left gaps impossible to fill. This was not the cheerful jumble of a flea market but the debris of lives destroyed by the new era. I recognized the worn china of a cup, the shape of the heels on a pair of shoes, the trademark on a transistor radio . . . These relics dated from my childhood. A whole epoch up for sale in these old hands, blue with cold.

More than all the other changes, more even than the obscene flaunting of the new wealth, it was this dispersal of a human past that struck me. The feverish speed with which it was being made to disappear. This dispersal and also the beauty of the child in her make-up. And my ignorance of what ought to be done in these new times to protect that child.

Siberia made me forget my botched homecoming. Here nothing had changed as yet. The handful of new republics, arisen from the collapse of the empire, had done no more than add colours to the geographers' maps. The earth remained the same: endless, white, indifferent to the rare appearances of men. Amid the torpor of winter they were not on the lookout for the latest upheavals in world news but for the russet streak of sunlight that would graze the horizon in a few days' time, after a long polar night.

Listening to the geologists in the *izba* at the Edge, I told myself that they came from the same epoch as those objects being sold by the old men in the corridors of the Metro. They lived as if the five thousand miles of snow that lay between them and Moscow had slowed down the passage of time. The sixties? The seventies? Everything in the way they lived, the way they talked, was twenty or thirty years out of date. That joke about the new arrival having sex with a bear . . . I had heard it more than once in my youth. Time here was twenty years slow. No, it was more like a time apart from time, a flow of days that took its tempo from the hissing of snow squalls against the window, the wheezing of the fire, the breathing of these three sleeping people, so different and so close: the two men with faces burned by the Arctic, the huge slant-eyed woman asleep in the room next door. (What are her dreams? Dreams where all is snow? Or on the contrary, filled with the sunlight of the South?). A nocturnal time, that took its rhythm from the throb of our blood in the arm crooked under the head, a warm pulse adrift in the endless white, amid the depths of this cosmic darkness, made iridescent by the Arctic phosphorescence.

Morning did not come. I was woken by a storm hurling flurries of snowflakes against the windows and filling the house with a dull vibration. It took me several seconds to grasp that this was due to a helicopter that had landed close beside the Edge. I saw light behind the mess-room door and heard the clatter of aluminium plates and mugs. The geologists got up in a hurry and even, it seemed to me, in a kind of panic. Big Lev sluiced his face furiously under the tap. Little Lev hastily wound up his clockwork razor . . .

The door yielded with a noisy crunch of shattered ice and now I thought I could guess the reason for their disarray. The man had to stoop as he made his way into the house and when he paused at the centre of the room, his face was level with the light bulb that glowed beneath the ceiling. He wore a black jacket of reversed sheepskin, and boots of reindeer hide. From his great height he studied the room, noted the disorder left by the previous night's bender but said nothing, waiting for the two Levs to come to him. This they did, greeting him with assumed nonchalance, but with shifty eyes: 'Good day to you, Chief!' 'Just five minutes, Captain, and we're ready!' Big Lev almost looked small. Little Lev had to reach up with his arm to shake the pilot's hand. The man eyed them in silence, then picked up the empty brandy bottle. 'I see you've been ready since yesterday,' he said in a deep voice, that sounded like the clutch being let in on an army cross-country vehicle on a bitterly cold day. 'I'm warning you, if I hear the slightest hiccup during the flight, I'll chuck you out, along with your firecrackers . . .'

The kitchen door opened, Valya came in carrying a huge kettle from which a wisp of steam emerged. I recalled my earlier astonishment: 'What man could make love to her?' Now her body seemed to take on normal proportions, the pilot's presence made her feminine, even seductive. 'Would you like a bite to eat?' she asked him. Smiling, he replied rather gruffly: 'No, we've no time. They've forecast wind at the end of the day . . . Just dose these two boozers with a bit of brine, otherwise they'll foul up the plane and half the Arctic . . .' He waved the brandy bottle and growled, still smiling: 'Look at this. They get themselves pissed on imported hooch these days. Bloody aristocrats . . .'

Then Little Lev intervened, trying to be conciliatory, and indicating me with one hand: 'This bottle, Chief.

You see it's our comrade from Moscow who brought it for us. But it's not strong at all! The thing is, if he could come with us this morning. He's a journalist . . .' The last sentence was uttered in increasingly faint tones and disappeared into a concluding stammer.

The pilot turned towards me and took me in with a hard look, though without hostility. 'The comrade from Moscow . . .' he murmured. 'First you get them drinking and now they're going to blow their own arses sky high instead of dynamiting the mountain.' He bent his head to go into the kitchen and added over his shoulder, as if the matter were settled, 'As for coming with us, very sorry. I don't do guided tours.'

Big Lev followed close behind him, avoiding my eye. Little Lev made a contrite face at me, spreading his arms in a gesture of helplessness.

I went out. The day was just beginning to dawn: an ashen grey light enabled one to make out the line of the mountains and, at my feet, a dwarf tree reached up towards the sky with its delicate, twisted branches, reminiscent of barbed-wire. In the half-light the helicopter was stirring up a slow flurry of flakes. I was an hour's flight away from my long journey's goal. Since leaving Paris I had travelled over seven thousand miles. Up there was the spot where Jacques Dorme's aircraft lay, somewhere at the heart of that icy mountain range. I could feel the cold (minus thirty-five? minus forty? the same as yesterday . . .) raking my face, breaking up my vision with the facets of tears. I suddenly grasped that it was essential to see that spot, that a writer's curiosity had nothing to do with it, that life had been secretly leading me towards this place and if I did not see it now my own life would be totally different.

The door grated. The two Levs emerged, laden with crates, made for the helicopter. I heard Valya's voice. The pilot paused on the threshold. I accosted him awkwardly, standing in his path: 'Listen, perhaps I could . . .' I saw the expression in his eyes, did not finish my sentence ('pay you?'). He gave me a pat on the shoulder and advised me, in more friendly tones: 'If I were you, I'd head straight for the village. There won't be another tractor until this evening . . .'

It was then that, in a lacklustre voice, reconciled to the setback and no longer asking for anything, I talked about Jacques Dorme. I managed to tell the story of his life in a few brief, bald sentences. I was in such a state of dejection that I scarcely heard what I was saying. And it was only in the state I was in that I was able to convey all the grievous truth of that life. A pilot from a remote country meets a woman from the same country and for a very few days, in a city which will soon be reduced to ruins, they are lovers; then he goes off to the ends of the earth to fly planes destined for the front and dies, crashing into an icy hillside under the pale sky of the Arctic Circle.

I told it differently. Not better but even more briefly, closer to the essence of their love.

The pilot took his hand off the door handle and murmured, as if in an effort of memory: 'Yes, I recall it now . . . It was that air bridge between Alaska and Siberia. The Alsib . . . They were real aces. They've almost been forgotten these days. That plane, it's not the one you can see on the Trident?' I nodded. The Trident, a mountain with three peaks . . .

'This is the last one, Chief. We're ready to go!' Little

Lev was coming down the front steps, a crate balanced on his shoulder.

The pilot gave a slight cough. 'And this woman. She was your . . .? Did you know her?' I spoke very softly, as if there were no one listening to me in this white desert. 'To me she was like a kind of . . . Yes, like a mother . . .'

'We're OK, Captain!' Big Lev's voice was cut off by the slamming of a door.

'Do you have papers on you?' asked the pilot, rubbing his nose. I thought about my passport written in a language he would not be able to read, and the note on it: 'any country except the USSR'.

'No, I'm . . . No. No papers . . .' He shook his head, and spread his hands wide, as if to say: 'In that case, there's nothing I can do for you.' Then suddenly he indicated his helicopter with a jerk of his chin, sighed and smiled: 'Right, come on then. Get in!'

As it took off, the aircraft banked and for the space of a second I saw the house on the Edge, the light in the kitchen window. It seemed to me as if the pilot had his eye on that window too.

Two and a half years after that secret journey my manuscript was complete. A much fictionalized account, for at the time I believed that only a novel could render the improbabilities of real life readable.

It was turned down by several publishers and then embarked on that ghostly but heady existence undergone by all texts that are repeatedly rejected: the life of a stillborn child or that of a spectre, periods in limbo interspersed with renewed hopes, with nights of feverish rereading, with disgust at the written word. The feeling of preaching in an over-populated wilderness. A dead-end whose extremity recedes the further down it you travel. A bottomless cul-de-sac.

I was halfway along this course when the receding of the dead-end seemed to come to a halt. I was in the office of an editorial director at one of the big Paris publishing houses, listening to such fervent praise that I feared a trap. In fact everything about this meeting was suspicious. I had expected to be confronted by a man of letters with thinning white hair, a fruity cough, his clothes steeped in tobacco, his body half buried beneath manuscripts, a real publishing animal. Yet here was a woman, seated with a lizard's elegance at a table where my text and nothing else occupied the place of honour. Petite, dark, with very intense, shining eyes, she was perched upon a tall, old-fashioned chair, so hard that a cushion was needed. Hers was the charm that a man may find provocative in a woman who is not his type but in whom he can see precisely what it is that might inspire passionate love in another man, the man he is not. This notion came to me later on. All I saw at the time was the movement of her lips, voicing a wildly enthusiastic opinion, without any publisher's reserve. I doubtless believed in the miracle of the preacher in the wilderness who is heard at last. This was my undoing.

I interrupted her (she was saying: 'What's so well done is the pair of them, the child and the old Frenchwoman telling him about her country and teaching him her language . . .'). I began to reveal the true story that lay behind the fiction. Odd scraps of life experience that only the plot of a novel could link together, scraps of love that only imagination could fashion into a love story, and a multitude of men and women who had had to be cast aside into oblivion . . .

'You see, the old Frenchwoman and her grandson, they were not actually . . .' I pressed on with what was in spite of myself fast becoming a work of demolition. I must have noticed this from the slight expression of pique that came over the woman's face. 'But all the characters are real people!' I concluded, as if offering the authentication of a vintage.

I do not know if she was aware that it was her plaudits that had lured me into this absurd outpouring. Her disappointment was that of a numismatist, who waxes lyrical over some old coins a navvy has brought in and holds forth elegantly about the time and place of their minting, and who suddenly sees the workman pick up a precious ducat and mark it with his tooth, to show that it is, indeed, gold.

Her tone did not change. 'Yes, quite . . . But what I meant to say to you was that, in the final section, especially, where you talk about the pilot, there are too many raw facts that have not been imaginatively reworked at all. And then there's the character of that general. That chance encounter . . .'

'But that's all true.'

'Precisely. And that's what jars. It's too true for a novel.'

I left, having been given a polite but firm ultimatum to the effect that I should rewrite the section in question.

The late retort, the *esprit de l'escalier*, occurred to me, not on the staircase, which was too narrow and hazardous for thoughts about literature, but on the curve of the pavement as I walked towards the rue du Bac. Amid a torrent of belated arguments what came to mind was the debate about truth and fiction unleashed by *War and Peace*. Murderous criticism, historians finding more than a thousand errors in the book and one newspaper's verdict: 'Even if this author had a shred of talent, he must still be condemned.' But especially the opinion of the old academician, Narov, who could not forgive Tolstoy for the degrading portrayal of Kutuzov, the Commander-in-Chief of the Russian forces. For on the eve of the decisive battle against Bonaparte at Borodino we see the saviour of Russia lounging in an armchair, a somewhat relaxed and extremely unmilitary posture, and to add insult to injury, immersed in a French novel! *Les Chevaliers du Cygne* (*The Knights of the Swan*) by Madame de Genlis . . . 'What kind of perverse imagination would create so false a scene?' thundered the academician. 'At that fateful hour Kutuzov would have been engaged in poring over battle maps – or at the very least, in reading Caesar's *Commentaries*.' Difficult to gainsay Narov, who took part in the battle and even lost an arm there. And yet . . . After Narov's death a good many French novels are found in his own library, among them *Les Chevaliers du Cygne*, with this note in handwriting on the flyleaf: 'Read in hospital, where I was nursing my wounds, after being taken prisoner by the French.'

For several seconds I regretted not having recounted this anecdote to the editorial director. But did the story, in fact, prove anything? Battle maps or Madame de Genlis? Perhaps quite simply the melancholy of an old man with only one year left to live, a man who has seen so many wars, so many victories and so many defeats and who 'at that fateful hour' lets his gaze stray into the serenity of a fine day in early September. He knows that tomorrow this calm will vanish beneath earth turned upside down by explosions, beneath the tramp of hundreds of thousands of men impatient to slit one another's throats, beneath the torrents of blood shed by the expected fifty to a hundred thousand victims. Then some time later the same calm will reign once more, the same sun will shine, the same gossamer threads will float on the air.

As I continued along the rue du Bac, I reflected that to escape from this childish equation, balancing real against imaginary, one should probably merely note down those utterly simple moments of human presence. Old Kutuzov's gaze at a window open onto the September sky . . . Nothing else.

*   *   *

I knew in advance that it would be impossible to touch up Jacques Dorme's life story. To make it more 'literary'? To what end? Impossible, too, to tamper with the figure of the general, the man for whom, according to the pilot, heaven would 'play a greater part than anything else'. That was the way the words had been reported to me, in isolation as a simple matter of fact. This French general was no more than a vague figure mentioned in a more or less chance conversation on a night rescued from oblivion thanks to a broken amber necklace. Why should it be necessary to tell it differently?

So I sacrificed these two men, tightened up the narrative, thinking somewhat ruefully as I did so of those group portraits in Stalin's era, from which, thanks to expert brushwork, the faces of leaders who had been shot used to disappear.

Wasted effort, because the text was rejected anyway, and later accepted elsewhere, published, enjoyed great success, exposed me to fleeting renown and to a surprisingly more tenacious resentment ('Do these immigrants think they can teach us to write French?' ruminated one Parisian critic), and finally relegated me to a new anonymity, infinitely preferable to the previous one because now without any illusions.

Towards the end of this whirlwind, however, I had an encounter indirectly linked to the two characters who had been sacrificed. A May evening in Canberra, autumn in Australia, a discussion with my readers (their irrepressible desire to know what is 'true' and what is fiction in the book). Then a conversation with a man in his thirties, the French cultural attaché, who has had the tact over dinner not to carry on where my readers left off, as people from embassies generally do; he lets me catch my breath and also talks very little about himself. Only after dinner, when we find ourselves under the sky with its strange array of constellations, does he talk, very simply, about the day of the general's death (he is his great-great-nephew and bears the same name, but has no reason to know what this name signifies in my own life). In any case he had not seen much that day, he was too young. An armoured personnel carrier, with the turret removed, bore the coffin up to the little church, a sober ceremony . . . Later, in school, the teacher asked them to write what they thought about the dead man.

As he talks to me, he evinces no desire to fire my imagination, recognizes that, being a child, he has re-membered only details, often trivial ones. I sense that I could add my own tale to his, but that to do so I should have to go back to the boy listening to the story of the snapped necklace and the pilot who flew over endless icy wastes, the boy who had seen the French general in the middle of the steppes beyond the Volga. For a moment I am on the point of coming out with it, and he seems to sense this past in me . . . Then we both remark on the beauty of the Southern Cross, particularly glorious on this autumn night, and part company.

# Two

What remains from that boyhood is an early morning in front of the half-open door of the sick bay. I am there, my hand poised to knock, I can already see the woman sitting inside, then, suddenly, this gesture: the woman squeezes her left breast, massages it, as if she were suffering from heartburn or were quite simply adjusting a brassiere too tight for that large breast. I knock and go in. She examines me and sets about washing the ugly scratch along my thigh. She is a young woman with slightly red hair, her movements are slow. I stay standing, towering over her; it is strange to be seeing an adult woman in this way, seeing her face bowed forwards, the apparent resignation in her eyes. When she looks up there is an admission of complicity between us. I leave the surgery unable to separate the mother from the woman in the one who has dressed my wound. Both intensely unknown, both intensely desired.

I had been hurt trying to hold back the orphanage's refuse bin on a waterlogged slope. Each morning a supervisor appears at the entrance to the dormitory, a list of names in his hand, and announces the fatigue duty. Always two names and, in response, a sotto voce muttering of oaths.

This time my partner was a youth despised by us all,

not for his weakness, which would have been logical in the enclosed world of the orphanage, where only strength counted, but for being like a peasant. Indeed, such was his rustic air, with his perpetually muddy shoes and his way of scratching his shaven head, that he was nick-named 'Village' . . . Without saying a word to him, I grasped one of the handles of the bin and we set about pushing this great steel container along a dirt road in the rain-sodden darkness of an autumn morning. Suddenly, we heard this voice behind us: 'Wait, take these as well!' On the threshold of the service door stood the librarian, with two great cardboard boxes at his feet. 'Take these to the boiler room . . .' Village went and fetched them, placed them on the lid of the bin, and pretended to set off again. But as soon as the door banged shut he stopped, threw me a wink and took hold of one of the boxes. 'You never know, there could be stuff to eat in there,' he explained. I had always thought him spineless, devoid of imagination . . . With a broad five-kopeck piece, sharpened into a cutting edge (the supervisors harried the possessors of knives relentlessly), he cut through the string, snapped back the cardboard flaps . . . 'Sod it! Just a lot of old books . . . Hang on. What's in the other one?' It was the same thing. Pamphlets, all with a photo on the covers we had no difficulty recog-nizing. The round, smooth face, the bald head: Khrush-chev, who had been overthrown the year before. Since then his portrait had disappeared from the fronts of buildings in the town and now, like a belated echo of events in Moscow, his 'Speech to the Twentieth Party Congress' was being withdrawn from provincial li-braries.

Seated in front of a stove's red-hot mouth, the heating engineer received the cardboard boxes impassively. He opened one of them, gave a rather sad little laugh and began throwing the pamphlets into the fire, one after the other. 'Oh Nikita, they were too clever for you, weren't they?' he observed, contemplating the auto-da-fé. 'And now the ones who've not been rehabilitated don't have a hope in hell . . .' Then, remembering us: 'Go on, get a move on, you kids. The bell's gone already . . .'

On the return journey Village asked me to wait for him and slipped into the undergrowth that covered the road-sides. I took several paces to distance myself from the stink of the bin. Up there on a hill the orphanage windows were strung out in a line: dark in the dormitories, lit up in the classrooms. You could even make out the figures of teachers in front of the blackboards. The only advantage of the refuse fatigue was that you were allowed to be a few minutes late.

'The ones who've not been rehabilitated . . .' The most widely shared and most jealously cherished myth among the pupils at the orphanage was precisely this: the hero-father, after being unjustly condemned, is finally rehabilitated; he returns, walks into the classroom, interrupts the lesson and inspires silent rapture in both the female teacher and the rest of the class. A handsome officer, his tunic ablaze with medals. There were other variants on this: fathers who were arctic explorers, fathers killed in battle, those who were submarine captains. But the return of the rehabilitated hero took precedence over all the other legends, for it was closer to the truth. It was the special function of this establishment to house the children of men and women who had distinguished them-

31

selves during the last war but who had subsequently proved unworthy of their heroic exploits. Such, at least, was the version communicated to us, sometimes with a degree of tact, it must be conceded, sometimes with all the venom of a supervisor in a rage: 'Like father, like son' . . .

'Look at them all grafting away, the little canaries!' Village had just appeared out of the darkness and was pointing up at the windows, where the heads of the pupils could be seen. 'Birds in a cage,' he added with mild scorn. We set off once more. At that time I did not fully understand what lay behind the heating engineer's words (we were eleven- and twelve-year-olds, Village must have been fourteen, for he had stayed down in the same class at least two years running), but I had grasped the main thrust: another era was beginning that would make our daydreams more unrealistic than ever. The handsome rehabilitated officer was going to remain forever outside the classroom door, would never bring himself to throw it open.

These thoughts distracted me and as we braced ourselves to heave the bin up a slope, I slipped and found myself on the ground with a gash on my thigh from the rusty steel. 'Lucky devil! That'll see you right for the day,' Village observed, feeling the wound. 'You should bugger off quick and see the nurse!'

So there was this day of rest, but above all the memory that obsessed me of a woman lifting her left breast and then of my own presence a few inches away from this woman, in the intimacy of a stolen secret.

Love makes us vulnerable. No doubt the ones who attacked me two days later had sensed in me the weakness of someone in love. All relationships at the orphange were governed by lines of force stretched to extremes. You had to maintain your position in the hierarchy of the strong and the less strong at all costs. Precisely as in a prison or in the underworld. I was neither one of the young gang leaders, of which there were several, nor one of the underdogs. Attacks were not made at random, moreover, for even the puniest of us might be clutching a thick five-kopeck piece sharpened into a razor-blade between his fingers.

During one break (I was gazing through the glass at the bare trees outside and telling myself that the nurse must be able to see them from her window too), a blow from someone's shoulder thrust me over against the wall, creating a space around me in the crowd of pupils, which quickly parted. It was a petty gang leader surrounded by his praetorian guard. His face, as is often the case with southerners, already had the texture of a man's and exhibited all the little grimaces of virility, all the tics of a young male who knows he is handsome. A few insults, to initiate the brawl, followed by hoots of laughter from the gang. Finally, in the middle of spitting out the scraps of tobacco that stuck to his lip, this sentence, in which his superiority found its ultimate expression, scornful and almost languid: 'Look, we all know about your father. The firing squad shot him like a dog . . .'

Every single one of our codes had been flouted. We often insulted and fought with one another, but we never tampered with the legend of the hero-fathers. I hurled myself at him, as he was already turning his back, leaving his henchman to deal with me. Others joined in, excited

33

by the general mêlée, happy to upgrade themselves in a pecking order suddenly thrown into disarray.

I was rescued by the appearance of a teacher at the end of the corridor. I stood up, hastily adjusting my shirt, which had lost several buttons, and wiping my nose which was bleeding. In our world aggressors and victims were punished without distinction.

In the toilets, with my face upturned under the icy jet from a tap, I gradually recovered my wits a little. As I waited for the bleeding to stop, I even had time to reflect on the sally that had imperilled all our legends: 'Your father gunned down like a dog . . .' Naturally this little warlord who was testing his virility knew nothing about the matter. Or rather, he knew that this tale would serve for every one of our fathers: lapsed heroes who had become mired in drink, crime or, worse still, dissidence, and who would end their days in a camp, or beneath the bullets of some guard perched high on his watchtower. He had said it out loud but for a while now we had all been aware that cracks were appearing in the heroic myth. And even without having listened to the old heating engineer's words as he burned Khrushchev, my fellow pupils could sense that the time when hope was still possible was drawing to a close. It was the middle of the sixties (November 1965, to be precise). Ill informed as we were, we did not know the word 'thaw', and yet we were, quite literally, the children of the Thaw. It was thanks to that bald, tubby man, whose books they were burning, that we lived in the relative comfort of an orphanage and not behind the barbed-wire of a re-education colony.

At the time I had a very confused grasp of all this. A

presentiment, a vague anxiety shared with the others. There was a kind of relief, too: it was not my lovesick demeanour that provoked the others' aggression. Quite simply, our little world was beginning to fall apart and one of the first fragments had just come and hit me in the face.

In a novel it would be possible to evoke many nuances to that day and the pain of that day, to invent the days that led up to it and followed it. But all that stays in my memory of it is the figure of a boy, standing beside the wall with his nose in the air, squeezing it between his thumb and index finger. The dirty little windows to the toilet area look out over a row of bare trees, the meander of a river, a muddy road. The boy smiles. It has just occurred to him that if all he had suffered had been a simple nosebleed he could have reported to the sick bay, gone in, asked for treatment . . . As in the scene he had dreamed of a thousand times. But his nose is hideously swollen. (Show it to the woman in her white coat? Never!) Another time, perhaps. Blood and pain suddenly seem marvellously linked to the promise of love. He relaxes his finger and thumb, wipes his face, listens. Outside the door, the silence of a long, empty corridor. Over there, gathered in their classrooms, are boys and girls who can still find refuge in their heroic lies. He has just lost the right to dream. The truth tastes of blood spat into the washbasin and the poignant beauty of the first snowflakes that he suddenly notices on the other side of the windowpane. Their white, stellar perfection swallowed up by the thick, rutted mud.

In memory's fragile truth there is also an autumn evening, a room lit by an old table lamp with a blue-green
shade, a woman with silvery hair sewing back buttons
onto my shirt, our two cups of tea, a book bound in stiff
covers with worn leather corners, in which I have just
read a sentence I shall still remember thirty years later
(although I do not know this at the time): 'Thus it fell out
that on the banks of the Meuse, almost as destitute of
money as when he had come from thence to Paris in the
first flush of youth, one of the purest and fairest soldiers
of old France gave his life for the three fleurs-de-lis . . .'

The woman gets up, pours the hot tea, puts another log
into the little iron stove in the corner of the room. I read the
sentence again, I almost know it by heart already. To think
about this warrior of days gone by reduces the pain caused
by the mockery relentlessly burning into me with its acid:
'Your father, shot like a dog . . .'

It would all be different in a made-up story. Tinged with
pointless exoticism: this house with its walls covered in
dark weatherboarding and its gloomy aspect in the
approaching dusk, a room hidden away in a warren
of apartments and shadowy staircases, a woman whose
origins are shrouded in mystery, this ancient French
book . . .

Yet nothing struck me as bizarre about that November evening. I had come, as I did every Saturday night on leave from the orphanage, to spend twenty-four hours at Alexandra's: the good fortune of those amongst us who had some unlikely aunt ready to welcome them. In my case it was this woman who had once known my parents. A foreigner? Most assuredly, but her origins had long since been blurred by the length and harshness of her life in Russia, by the devastation of the war, which cut off those who had survived it from their past, from their nearest and dearest, from their own former selves. Also living in this great wooden house, moreover, were a family of Germans from the Volga, an ageless Korean (the victim of one of those population transfers which were an obsession of Stalin's) and, in a long, narrow room on the ground floor, a Tatar from the Crimea, Yussuf, the joiner, who had one day remarked to the woman who took me in, this woman born near Paris: 'You know, Shura, you Russians . . .' Her French Christian name had also undergone a slow process of Russification, becoming first of all 'Shura', then slipping into the affectionate diminutive 'Sasha', and finally reverting to the full name of 'Alexandra', which had no connection at all with her real Christian name.

Only the books she had bit by bit taught me to read still betrayed her imperceptible French origins. 'Thus he gave his life for the three fleurs-de-lis . . .'

A novelist's way of evoking this apprenticeship would no doubt link together a series of boyhood surprises in order to relate the story of an 'éducation française'. But in reality the most surprising thing was the natural way in

37

which, having arrived at the big wooden house, I would climb its dark staircases, open Alexandra's door, put my bag down on a chair. I vaguely knew the house's history: a certain Venedikt Samoylov, who was engaged in the wool trade with Central Asia before the Revolution, had built what at the beginning of the century was a small manor house of pale wood; he had been expelled from it and disappeared, leaving behind a rich library that soon fell victim to the hungry stoves installed by new inhabitants in the increasingly dilapidated rooms. During the war the house, being located in a small township near Stalingrad, had been partly destroyed by an incendiary bomb, had lost one of its wings and at the time of my childhood still displayed a broad stretch of charred wall.

The truth of memory compels me to recognize that I found neither these blackened timbers nor the extreme poverty of the rooms surprising. Nor did I notice their caravanserai exoticism. I climbed the stairs, drinking in with pleasure the smells that only family life can produce, a mixture of cooking and laundry; I walked past the inhabitants, happy to feel that I was their equal, for I was now liberated from my regimented existence; I went into Alexandra's room (the aroma of good tea could already be detected in the icy darkness of the staircase) and it felt like a definitive return, like going back to a house that awaited me, one I should not have to leave the following day. I was home at last.

In my adult life since then I have never rediscovered the same feeling of permanence . . .

In the course of these visits I had certainly received a French education. But an education without structure, unpremeditated. A book left open on the corner of a table, a Russian word whose French past Alexandra revealed to me . . . The feeling of being home at last mingled imperceptibly with this foreign language I was learning. The association became so intense that for me many years later the French language would always be evocative of a place and a time that came close to the atmosphere of the childhood home I had never known.

She had begun to teach me her language because, in the extreme poverty of our lives then, it was the last remaining treasure she could share with me. An evening with her, from time to time, that gave me the illusion of family life. And this language. There was probably a moment that first triggered things, a word, a story, something arousing my curiosity, I no longer remember. But I remember very well the day I managed to get into a little room cut off from the rest of the house by that fire in the spring of 1942. For twenty years this cubby-hole, tucked away under the rafters, had remained inaccessible, sealed off by the thick planks the inhabitants had nailed up where the wall had been breached. The door to this tiny room led to the outside, to the empty space where the wing had collapsed. To reach it I had climbed out through the landing window. This acrobatic feat was not without risk, as I had to cling to the remnant of a beam, place my foot on the skirting of a floor that had vanished and, squeezing the whole of my body against the charred wood, grasp the door handle. Inside I had discovered the remnants of Samoylov's library, piles of books damaged by fire, age and rain. Foreign books especially, useless to the building's residents and saved from their stoves thanks to this room being sealed off. I had brought some of them back from my perilous expedition. Alexandra had scolded me (I was barely seven years old) and then shown me her own books. Did they, too, come from the ruined library or from a more distant past? I do not know. All that comes back to me now is this moment: pressed flat against the blackened timbers, I reach my hand out towards the handle, suddenly see my reflection in a mirror with a tin frame hanging on the wall, realise that the void, along the edge of which I am sidling, was once an inhabited room, have time to stare at my own face. An instant of my life, the extreme singularity of this instant, a sky in which snow floats down very slowly, almost motionless.

My French education resembled the efforts of a palaeontologist to reconstruct a vanished world, starting from discovered bones. The isolation in which our country lived at that time turned the French universe into a landscape as mysterious as that of the Cretaceous or the Carboniferous eras. Every novel on Alexandra's shelves became the vestigial remains of a vanished – not to say extraterrestrial – civilization, a fossil, a droplet of amber that held within it not an imprisoned insect but some character, a French town, a district of Paris.

In the ensuing years Alexandra made me read some of the classics, but it was thanks to the little sealed-off room that my sense of being engaged in exploration was at its most vivid. I found many French books there, some of them eaten away by damp and now unreadable, some of them printed with the old spelling of verbs in the imperfect tense ending in 'oit', instead of 'ait', which confused me at first. In one of these abandoned volumes I came across an anecdote that made a greater impression on me (I have long been ashamed to admit) than the work of many a famous novelist. It concerned the actress Madeleine Brohant, celebrated in her day, but who lived out her last years in great penury, lodging on the fourth floor of an ancient block of flats in the rue de Rivoli. One of the rare friends who remained faithful to her complained breathlessly on one occasion, about the exhausting climb. 'But my dear friend,' replied the actress, 'this staircase is all I have left to make men's hearts beat faster!' The most glittering alexandrines, the most cunningly plotted novels would never teach me more about the nature of Frenchness than that gentle, wry remark, whose rhythmic resonance, it seems to me, I can still hear.

Was there any logic to this apprenticeship? A work of fiction could easily conjure up the stages in it, the progress made, the things learned. My memory only retains a handful of moments or apparently unconnected insights. Madeleine Brohant's remark and, also, that day in the troubled and tempestuous life of the Duchesse de Longeville. When they brought her a glass of water the adventuress, parched with thirst, hurled herself upon it and declared, with a voluptuous sigh: 'Such a shame this is not a sin!'

And yet there was a connection, all the same, between these fragments preserved in the memory. The art of eloquence and epigram, the cult of sense turned on its head, word play that made reality less absolute and judgements less predictable. In those days Russian life still resonated with echos of Stalin's time: 'enemy of the People' and 'traitor to the Country' had not really gone out of use. At the orphanage, indeed, despite our day-dreams of heroes, we knew that our fathers had been described in precisely those terms. Once poured into the mould of propaganda, words had the hardness of steel, the heaviness of lead. As he burned Khrushchev's pamphlets, the old heating engineer had muttered the phrase 'arbitrary voluntarism' (an official accusation he must have heard on the radio and had difficulty in articulating), as if it were the complicated name of a shameful disease. We did not know what it meant but we felt an obscure respect for the power of this 'ism', which had just brought down the country's top man and compelled our teachers to steer clear of certain passages in our textbooks.

Unconsciously, perhaps, I drew a parallel between this steely language and the lightness of the glass of water that became a sin on the Duchesse de Longeville's lips, or the airy sweetness of an arduous staircase that caused hearts to beat faster. Words that killed and words that, when used in a certain way, liberated.

This contrast had led me one day to Alphonse Martinville . . . My fingers grimy with soot, I was laying out volumes that often fell to pieces in my hands. Framed in the doorway of the abandoned room was a spring sky, tender and luminous, and yet the pages of the book I had discovered beneath a bundle of old newspapers quivered with jacobinic fury and the clatter of the guillotine. It was Year II of the Revolution and the crowd thirsted for blood. On the fifteenth of the month of Ventôse, the March rain came streaming off the blade of the machine onto the scaffold. Which they had no time now to wash down. A young condemned man appeared: 'Stand before us, Alphonse de

42

Martinville!' ordered the presiding judge. Surprised to be awarded an aristocratic 'de', the young man retorted with a desperado's courage: 'But I have come here to be made shorter – not longer.' This sally won over the crowd and pleased the tribunal. A cry went up: 'Citizens! Release him!' The rejoicing was general. Martinville was acquitted.

Among all these books, I have remembered some rather against my will on account of the notes in purple ink in the margin. In particular one very heavily annotated one: *Will the Human Race Improve?* I was at an age when this title did not yet seem comical. I spent a long time studying the elegant 'NB's and 'sic's added by the former owner of the house, the merchant Samoylov, the doughty auto-didact, whom I pictured in his study of an evening, with big round spectacles perched on his nose, his brow creased, running his finger along sentences penned by a long forgotten French thinker.

But as it happens, more than the great classics and the vicissitudes of History, it was a textbook in French dealing with various processes used for tempering blades that for a long time fascinated me. I spent hours decipher-ing the methods described (as I recall: powdered graphite mixed with oil . . .), trying to construct the replica of a dagger that bore the exciting name of *Misericordia*. The book gave details of its origin and use. When an unseated knight, protected by his armour, refused to yield, re-course was had to this long, slender blade 'that pierced the heart like a scorpion's sting'.

The French education I was receiving was really not all that academic.

*   *   *

This particular November evening was like all the others and utterly different. I had ended up telling Alexandra about the fight in which I was confronted by the others, their mocking taunts: '. . . your dad, gunned down like a dog.' She broke off from her task of sewing the buttons back onto my shirt, laid it down on the table and began talking very naturally about my parents, going back over the story I already knew fragments of: their flight, their settling in the north of the Caucasus, my birth, their death . . .

In a novel, the child would perforce have listened to such an account with grief-stricken attention (how many books would I subsequently read, often pathetic and lachrymose, about the quest for family origins). But in fact I was sunk in a dull insensibility and followed it with a kind of resigned deafness. Alexandra noticed this, no doubt understanding that what counted for me, for all of us at the orphanage, was not the truth of the facts (broadly speaking similar for all our parents), but the grand legend of an officer unjustly condemned, who would one day throw open the classroom door. She persevered, however, knowing that what she confided to me was being inscribed in my memory without my knowing it and might thus escape being forgotten.

I listened to her distractedly, from time to time glancing at the pages of the book open in front of me, at the sentence I preferred to all the truths of reality: 'Thus it fell out that . . . one of the purest and fairest soldiers of old France gave his life for the three fleurs-de-lis . . .'

The brawl that had made it impossible for me to picture a heroic father also had another consequence. Some days later there was this bone that one of the pupils fished up from his plate and threw across the refectory table in my direction. His shout: 'Here. Give the dog a bone!' was followed by an outburst of laughter from the whole table and immediately afterwards a tense silence, everyone looking down at their food: a supervisor had just appeared at the door. 'What do you think you're doing, throwing filth about?' he said angrily, pointing his finger at the bone that had landed near my plate. 'No supper tonight! You can clean the corridor outside the Lenin Room. I don't want to see a speck of dirt left there!'

In the solitude of this long corridor that led to 'the Lenin Room' (part museum, part treasure house, which honoured the great man's memory in every school in the country), I felt almost happy. With that happiness that follows the extinguishing of all hope and teaches us that in the end every grief is bearable. The wet floorboards reflected the light of the single lamp at the end of the corridor. Dazed by the toing and froing of the floorcloth, it was as if, beneath the dark, watery surface, my gaze were discovering the illusory depths of a secret world.

The task finished, I lugged the bucket along to the toilet area. As I washed my hands I noticed brown stains on the wall around the tap. They were the dried specks of my blood, traces of the fight three days before. There I had bled and with wistful tenderness had thought about the woman massaging her left breast . . . I threw water over the soiled place, rubbing it hastily, as if someone might have been able to divine its mystery.

For a while I remained in the storage room where the cleaning women kept their brushes and where I had put away my bucket. I liked this place: boxes of brown soap that gave off a pleasant musky smell, a narrow fanlight open onto a freezing night, my body pressed against the radiator that warmed my knees through the cloth of my trousers . . . My personal space. It was precisely on that evening that I became aware of it: a tiny island where the world was not an open wound. Away from it, everything hurt. In a claustrophobic reflex, no doubt, I was racking my brains for an escape, a continuation of these moments of tranquillity, an archipelago of brief joys. I recalled one of the last readings at Alexandra's house. I had come across an unfamiliar French word, 'estran', meaning 'foreshore'. She had explained its meaning to me in French. I had pictured this strip of sand liberated by the waves and, without ever having seen the sea, I had a perfect sense of being there, studying everything the ocean leaves behind on a beach as it retreats. I now understood that this 'estran', for which I did not know the word in Russian, was also my life, just like the fourth floor of that ancient block of flats where Madeleine Brohant lived.

It was probably on that evening that I first perceived with such clarity what it was that Alexandra's language had given me . . .

The door opened abruptly. The intruder had the air of

one coming home. It was Village. He stared at me, vexed, but not fiercely. 'So you're the one who's been spilling all that water down the corridor. I slid ten yards along it on my arse. It's worse than an ice rink . . .' Under his coat he was clutching a bundle wrapped in a sheet of newspaper. The cool of the snow that he had brought in with him stood out clearly from a very appetising, smoky smell that made me swallow my saliva and reminded me I had eaten nothing since midday. Village noticed my famished grimace and gave a satisfied smile. 'So, did they not give you a scrap to eat, the two-faced sods?' he asked, taking off his jacket.

'No, nothing,' I choked, in another contraction of the throat, surprised by this description of the others.

'Ah well, tough on them. They get the same grub every single day. Enough to give a cockroach the trots. Now you and me are going to enjoy this . . .'

In the twinkling of an eye he transformed the cubby-hole into a dining-room. The lid of a crate laid over a bucket formed the table. Two other buckets, upturned, became chairs. From out of the folded newspaper a grilled fish made its appearance, with a broad, curved body, its fins blackened by the fire . . . We began to eat . . . Village told me tales of his secret fishing trips, his tricks for escaping from the orphanage. From time to time, he cocked an ear, then resumed his talk, speaking more softly . . . At the end of our meal footsteps outside the door gave us a start. A supervisor's voice called out my name. Village stood up, handed me a bucket, opened the door and hid behind it.

'What are you doing in there?' the man demanded, patting the wall, but not finding the switch.

'Well, I was just putting the bucket away, that's all,' I replied with a rough assurance that surprised even myself.

The supervisor, still in the half-light, sniffed the air, but the supposition that came to him seemed so far-fetched that he withdrew, growling: 'Right. Put all that stuff away and quickly to bed.' Squeezed behind the door Village gave me the thumbs up: 'Well acted there!'

Up on the dormitory floor, before we went our separate ways, this is what he said to me, with the shaky intonation that betrays words deeply buried, which it is painful suddenly to give voice to: 'You know . . . my dad, they . . . shot him too. With a comrade. He was trying to escape . . . But the guard spotted them and gunned them down. An old man once told me that in the camps, when fellows were killed trying to escape, they left them in full view for three days, in front of the barrack huts, so the others knew what to expect . . . When my mother heard the news she took to drinking. And when she died the doctor he said it was like she was burned from the inside. And just before she went, she kept saying to me: "It was to see you he did that." But I never believed her, you know . . .'

The laconic friendship that bound us together taught me a lot. The most despised pariah in the orphanage, Village was in reality the most free of us all. Almost every day he was to be seen engaged on the refuse fatigue, but what we did not know was that he volunteered for it and could thus spend long, stolen moments pacing up and down on the banks of the river, sometimes venturing as far as the Volga. He was also the only one to accept reality, not to invoke the phantom of the officer who was going to come knocking at the classroom door. What he did not accept was the reality they constructed for us, with its myths, its lapsed heroes, its books burned in the boiler-room stove. And while we were lined up class by class in the corridor, before lessons started, listening, without listening, to the singsong ranting of the loud-speaker ('The party of Lenin, a people's force, leads us on to the triumph of Communism!'), Village was slipping through the willow plantations in the morning mist, in the fragile awakening of the waters fringed with the first ice. That was his reality.

I told myself that my '*estran*' was not so far removed from Village's misty mornings.

The land of the '*estran*', a land of refuge, where it was still possible for me to dream, revealed itself bit by bit, without any logic, amid the relics of Samoylov's library. It was there, one day, that a torn page, marked by the fire, came to hand; on it the opening lines of a poem, whose author I was never able to identify:

> When upon Nancy the sun doth rise
> Already he's shining in Burgundy's skies.
> He'll soon be here to start our day,
> Then onto Gascony make his way.

No geography would ever give me a more concrete sense of the land of France, a territory that had always seemed to me much too tiny on the maps to have pretensions to time zones. What the poet had expressed was his feeling for the beloved space, a physical perception of one's native land that enables us to take in a whole country at a single glance, to perceive its tonalities very distinctly, as they differ from one valley to the next, the variation in landscapes, the unique substance of each of its towns, the mineral texture of their walls. From Nancy to Gascony . . .

I did not feel as if I were in pursuit of any goal as I explored the ruins of these books in the sealed-off room. Mine was the simple curiosity of one who pokes about in attics, the pleasure of lighting upon a book spared by the fire, an unblemished engraving, a note calligraphed in the old style. The joy, above all, of coming down, my arms piled high with these treasures, and showing them to Alexandra. Yet shortly after reading those four lines of verse on that torn-out page I grasped what it was that drove me to spend long hours in the company of these mutilated books. From the bottom of a box where the wood was disintegrating like sand, I drew out a *History of the Late Roman Empire* with the pages stuck together by damp, then a book in German, printed in flamboyant Gothic lettering and finally, from a collection of texts with its cover missing, an obituary notice. I no longer remember whom it concerned. The shade of a great, vanished lineage is linked, all too confusedly, with my reading of this. All I can remember, but I recall them by heart, are the words of François I, quoted by the author, which were underlined in that violet ink whose faded tint I recognized: 'We are four noblemen from Aquitaine, who will fight in the lists against all comers from France: myself, Sansac, Montalembert and la Châtaigneraie.' I pictured that country, encompassed by a loving gaze that followed the sun's course from Nancy to Gascony, knowing now that it was the gaze of these four knights scanning their native land, the better to defend it.

What I was searching for in my reading was what I lacked. Attachment to a place (that of my own birth was too ill defined), a personal mythology, a family past. But, above all, that thing of which the others had just robbed me: the divine freedom to reinvent life, and to people it with heroes. For me the four knights of Aquitaine were much more real than those ghosts of handsome officers that haunted the orphange dormitories.

Did I really believe in these equestrian figures standing guard over France? I think I did, just as at the age of eleven or twelve one believes in nobility, compassion, self-sacrifice. After all, it was not the reality of this vision that interested me, but its beauty. A road high on a hillside, the dust muffling the clatter of the hooves, the four companions advancing slowly, their gaze directed into the distance, now towards the mountains, clustered in the mists, now towards the gap where the ocean glistened. That was how I saw them, it was my way of hoping.

One day this land I dreamed of finally imprinted its space within me, as the pattern of the constellations imprints itself in our visual memory, and the ups and downs of a familiar path do in the soles of our feet. I became aware of this during the last literature lesson before the New Year holidays. The atmosphere was not very studious. Some of us were dozing, hypnotized by the swirling of great snowflakes outside the window, others at the back of the class were choking with whispered laughter as they passed a textbook from hand to hand beneath the desks, open at a disfigured illustration. From time to time the voice of the teacher, a tall, bony woman with a heavy, prominent chin, thundered out: 'Who wants to go without food until tomorrow?' The class would freeze, she would resume her dissection of a poem by Lermontov, and the textbook provoked new spasms of hilarity. When I set eyes on it I could not help smiling. The poem we were studying (dedicated to Napoleon) was illustrated with the painting that shows the emperor just after his abdication. An unfortunate choice, if one knows the penchant naughty schoolboys have for desecrating images of famous people in textbooks. Napoleon was seated, with a downcast air, his body shrunken, his gaze fixed, his legs wide apart. And it was in this space between the imperial legs that a sacrilegious hand had drawn a monstrous hairy tube adorned with two enormous balls. Another, more innocent hand had covered his face with long, stitched up scars, hidden his left eye behind a pirate's patch. I smiled, reflecting that some famous people in our textbooks acquired even more infamous addenda, even more muscular appendages . . . It was at that moment that the teacher began to declaim the poem.

She read it both badly and well. Badly, because her voice was monotonous and evidently alert to the somnolence of some and the giggling whispers of the rest. Well, because the banality of this voice enabled me to forget it, to forget this tall woman with her angular frame, to forget this classroom, to enter into the nocturnal world of these stanzas, to find myself on an island lost in the middle of an ocean, beside a stone tomb that opens once a year, at midnight on the anniversary of the emperor's death. The dead man arises and climbs aboard the ghost ship, which sets sail for 'that beloved France where he had left his glory, his throne, his son and heir and his faithful Guard.' He lands by night and rouses the deserted shore with a powerful call that reverberates into the very depths of the country. But his native land remains deaf: 'The moustached grenadiers are all asleep now on the plain where the Elbe's waters flow, beneath the snows of cold Russia, in the burning sands of the pyramids.' Then he summons his marshals: 'Ney! Lannes! Murat . . .' No one comes to his side. 'Some have fallen in battle, others have betrayed him and sold their swords.' With a despairing cry he calls out to his son, but in reply hears only the deathly silence of the void. Dawn compels him to leave his native land. He boards the ghost ship and it carries him back to his remote island.

I had never before had such a feeling of freedom in the face of reality. The beauty of this nocturnal voyage rendered the so-called real world all around me so insignificant that I wanted to laugh: the walls of this classroom, decorated with strips of red calico bearing quotations from Lenin and the last Party Congress: the orphanage building; the chimneys of a vast factory beyond the icebound river. The man who stood on the deck of that spectral ship, this figure in its tricorne hat, had nothing to do with the Bonaparte whose adventures we learned about from our history books, nor with the 'literary personage' analysed by our teacher, nor with that fat little man with his legs apart, portrayed in the illustration. The exile returning to the shores of Brittany, sending out his calls to his marshals, was a reality divined by the poet. More true than History itself. More believable because it was beautiful.

I knew the voyager on the ghost ship belonged to the land of the four noblemen from Aquitaine, and that he could, like them, encompass it in a single look, from the forests of the east to the dunes beside the ocean. When the hinged lids of our old desks came clattering down at the end of the lesson I reflected that it might somehow be possible never to lose contact in my mind with this dreamed-of land.

According to the logic of my adolescent quest, I should have plunged into an increasingly disdainful and un-tamed solitude and adopted the posture of the young king in exile. A being torn between his dreams of France and reality. A logic both novelistic and romantic. But it all turned out differently. It was reality that suddenly produced a dramatic twist in the plot.

At first it was just a rumour, so improbable that, talking about it during the New Year holidays, we treated it as a bizarre hoax. Our holidays, in any case, were not like those of normal schoolchildren. We would be sent out to clear railway lines, often blocked by snowstorms, or else from time to time we were lined up in a guard of honour on the occasion of some official visit. Our city's glorious past attracted foreign delegations. Lining the perimeter of a monument to the fallen, we represented 'Soviet youth, assembled in evergreen commemoration of the war'. It was especially during the holidays that they had recourse to us because at such times normal children were difficult to mobilize. Or when it was particularly cold, too, since parents would refuse to expose their little ones to snowstorms at minus twenty-five.

That December it was indeed very cold. Despite being ordered to stand to attention, we jumped up and down in our ranks, the soles of our ancient shoes thumping on the ice, and to warm the cockles of our hearts while waiting for the official procession to pass, we discussed this stupid rumour. What joker could have started it?

When lessons resumed the news broke. The rumour was true: next autumn the orphanage was going to close.

In the months that followed we learned the details: the pupils would be transferred to ordinary boarding schools, the older ones to technical establishments and factories, possibly even in distant towns. But we only really believed it all in June, when, after lessons had finished, they ordered us to drag our old desks over to the boiler-room. Right up to that day we went on clinging to the hope that it was all a false alarm. And yet each one of us, in his own way, was making ready to leave.

The orphanage, the equivalent of the prison into which our fathers had vanished, suddenly took on a different character, revealing its hospitable, almost familial side to us. The lives led by other people, whose freedom we had always envied, now alarmed us. We were like the prison inmate at the end of a long sentence, counting the hours and at the same time dreading going outside, who often escapes just before the great day, allows himself to be caught and settles down to a new total of days to be crossed off.

To outward appearances our daily life remained the

same. The most noticeable change was a kind of solidarity that imposed itself of its own accord, cancelling out the former hierarchies of weak and strong. Strength, hostile and unknown, now lay outside our walls.

One Saturday evening in January I went up to the sealed-off room where I had almost finished sorting through the books. In the half-light their worlds came to life, their words resonated softly in my ears. On one of the boxes lay the blade of the future dagger, *Misericordia* . . . Alexandra called to me from the landing. I took a last look about me, thinking that I should soon have to leave these books behind for a long time, perhaps for ever, and that I must try to carry away within me the land that had been born from their pages.

# Three

That winter marked a hiatus between two generations, the notorious 'twenty years after', which, though too vague for historians, nevertheless sets the rhythm of a country's chronology. The war's end was already twenty years old. A generation had had the time to be born, grow up and produce offspring. All without war. Blood ties to it were being stretched, the heritage of memory was collapsing, the dead were taking on solid shape once and for all in bronze. That was precisely the time when they began erecting a forest of monuments in our city, vast concrete memorials in celebration of the battle of Stalingrad, colossal statues, and lighting 'everlasting flames'. And they closed our orphanage, with the view that the quarantine had lasted long enough, we had expiated our fathers' past, and it would now be ideologically more judicious to disperse us, like fragments from that past, among the healthy population.

The last months before our departure were filled in equal measure with excitement and anxiety. We knew that the myth of the hero-fathers could not fail to raise smiles among the people in whose midst we should soon be living. Not only did we come from a strange place but also from another era, from those days when the statues still moved and spoke, warm with the blood that flowed beneath the bronze. We would all, we knew very well, have to make up for lost time, find a place for ourselves in other people's reality. Learn to forget.

What I am left with from those months is a few brief fragments, snapshots in the memory, apparently random, but without which I should certainly have become a different person. Notably that January afternoon, a biting cold that forces us, despite being ordered to remain still, to rub our noses and lips, which have lost all feeling. The motorcade we are waiting for on one of the great avenues of the city is delayed. Everyone shuffles their feet to avoid turning into pillars of ice: the militiamen stationed several yards apart, ourselves behind them, along with other representatives of the 'toiling masses'. According to the rumour circulating, a very important person is expected, there are murmurs around us that it is Brezhnev himself. Our curiosity is aroused by the desire to guess which of the cars in the motorcade this person will travel in. Not the one at the head, we are sure of that. The second, the third? A state secret. We feel we have been entrusted with a mission. And still the motorcade is not there. Our feet seem to be ringing like lumps of ice. Irritated, one of the pupils from the orphanage tells a whispered joke. Wafted along on the breeze, it warms our ears. An attempt on Brezhnev's life. The gunman misses, is arrested, interrogated: 'So what stopped you shooting straight?' 'The crowd. They were all trying to shoot first.' Laughter unfreezes our lips. The militiamen look round. A supervisor looms up behind us, cuffs heads rapidly . . . The motorcade sweeps past at such a speed that it is impossible to get a good look at the windows in this black stream of limousines. Our hands spring into action too late, merely saluting the motorcyclists who bring up the rear. They have helmets white with hoar-frost and ruddy faces . . . The 'toiling masses' break ranks and disperse, hastening towards home and a hot drink. But our own mission is not yet accomplished. We are put on a bus and taken to the foot of a brand new monument, to act out the same charade of popular jubilation all over again, in Potemkin style. The wind from the steppes on this hillside is appalling. They arrange us in a hollow square, doubtless in simulation of a large crowd. We no longer talk, remain motionless, without the supervisors having to rebuke us. Even they seem to understand the inhuman absurdity of this wait-ing. The day wanes, the motorcade does not come. An NCO approaches our ranks, speaks into a supervisor's ear. The latter smiles at us a little mournfully: 'At ease!'

At this moment I take to my heels. Everyone is too tired to count us. I make my way down the other side of the hill, run towards the city. I do not explain to myself the reasons for this truancy. Possibly contempt for this visiting VIP, who has not deigned to come. Or else the picture I have of the rest of the extras, who have already gone home, happily drinking hot cups of tea in the bosom of their families. Probably the latter thought. The dazzling vision of this domestic bliss, warmth, peace. I make my way through the streets, mimicking the gait of the passers-by, I go into a shop. Then pause for a moment, mingling with the gathering at a bus stop, with the ill-considered hope that their life will draw me into itself, make me like them. A screen like a fine sheet of glass separates me from these people . . . I find myself inside a church, with no particular end in view, simply to get warm. My rejection of everything connected with religion is instinctive. I do not like these old women crossing themselves and mumbling in front of the icons wreathed in smoke. The reverberation beneath the vaulted ceilings is unpleasant, chilling. The gleaming richness of the iconostasis is crushing. And even the candle flames are no good for unfreezing my fingers, they burn them, bite them or else shrink away beneath them. I recall how one day at the orphanage one of the pupils was made to step forwards to be castigated for his shameful crime: some reactionary old aunt of his had secretly taken him to the church and had him baptized! Our contempt for this tearful redhead had been sincere. 'It was one of these old women here,' I say to myself, at the sight of their bowed shadows. The priest's voice is slightly plaintive, quavering with cold. I find his prayers hard to follow. He calls on us to pray for all and sundry, to pray for everyone, for those close at hand, for those far away, for the dead . . . I get back to the orphanage just before supper. I cannot admit to anyone that my first attempt to live among the others has failed.

Nor would I have become the person that I am without having experienced a certain night at the end of the winter. Or rather that particular moment when for a very brief spell the passing of the trains that ran beside the house where Alexandra lived came to a stop. During the day the tracks, only a few yards distant from the wooden walls, gave rise to the noisy symphony of trains on their way through the township. The inhabitants no longer even noticed all this pounding, clattering, whistling and grinding, the crescendos and diminuendos. Just from the sound they could recognize the heavy drumming of a train coming from the Urals, its trucks loaded with ore, the shock wave raised by the Novosibirsk express, the interminable clanking of the dark tank-wagons bringing oil from the Caspian Sea . . . Round about two o'clock in the morning there was a slack period in this rail activity, a brief respite between the very late trains and the ones that roused the marshalling yard at the crack of dawn. Sometimes this pause in the night was shattered by special trains passing through at high speed. As I lay in my bed, separated off from the rest of the room by an old curtain, all I had to do was crane my neck to see the long, low flatbed trucks rolling past, the transport covers that allowed one to guess at the contours of armoured vehicles, the shapes of guns. Then I remembered the things our teachers used to tell us about the world situation. These armaments were probably on their way to the defenders of Vietnam, currently being burned with napalm by the Americans, or to the Cubans, at their last gasp, thanks to the blockade, or to the Africans in their liberation struggle. The cause seemed to me just. I loved being woken by these trains shrouded in mystery.

That night I missed the passing of the nocturnal train. I sat up in bed as the last of the flatcars was already slipping by under the window. All I could make out was the unusual size of the devices being transported: the covers reached up higher than our first floor. 'Maybe they're rockets . . .' I thought, still half asleep, and remained like that for a while, listening to the slow fading of the sound. The night, as so often after the February thaws, was icy and clear. In the upper part of the window, where the fronds of hoar-frost had not made inroads, the darkness gleamed like clean-cut granite flecked with mica. Between two stalactites of ice that hung from the gutter a star stood out clearly, alive and aware of our lives, of the existence of this old wooden house, suspended in total isolation, in the somewhat terrifying splendour of this animated sky.

The final reverberations of the rails fell silent, the stillness was about to become absolute. And it was then that I became aware of a barely perceptible murmuring that continued to cloud the settling silence. I pricked up my ears and recognized Alexandra's voice, or rather the shadow of Alexandra's voice. The ceiling was faintly tinged with the glow of her night-light. Embarrassed at overhearing this whispering, I was about to get back into bed when I suddenly thought I heard my name. 'Perhaps she's having a heart attack,' I thought, 'and hasn't the strength to call out to me . . .' Anxious, but not wanting to give myself away, I delicately pushed aside the tired satin of the curtain . . . In the corner of the room, on the other side of the wardrobe that formed my cubby-hole, I saw an old woman seated on her bed, her feet, below a long night-dress, resting on a small rectangle of carpet. At first she seemed like a stranger. Her white hair was undone and reached her shoulders. Most strikingly there was her pose: her head deeply bowed, her fingers pressed against her brow. Among her faint, tremulous words I once more caught my name . . .

I did not think, I did not say to myself: 'A woman saying her prayers.' What occurred to me at that moment was much less considered. My whole being was filled with an awareness of the infinite night in which our house was adrift, the depth of the darkness, of the icy expanses of sky and earth, and, at the heart of this gaping space, a woman, giving voice to my presence in the universe.

The night-light went out. I lay there, unsleeping. Amid the early morning uproar of the trains, it struck me that she had been murmuring those secret words in her mother tongue.

During the days that followed, when I had managed to find the language to understand that night, I recalled the priest's litany, his quavering voice that had displeased me. Among others, he had called on us to pray 'for those who have no one to pray for them'. This form of words, incomprehensible to me at the time, now seemed poignantly apt. Knowing nothing about religious practice, I saw prayer as broadly speaking the act of thinking about a person, picturing them lost and isolated under the sky, and by this thought reaching them, even if they were unaware, especially if they were unaware of it.

'. . . Who have no one to pray for them.' In the grey light of a dawn slow to appear, I helped Village to retrieve his fishing lines, all of them without a catch. So the little wood fire he had just lit would serve no purpose. 'The months with an "r" in them are no bloody use for fishing,' he explained, making light of it. We had, in fact, reached the first days of March. The setback did not seem to affect him. He sat down on the carcass of an old boat, took out a hunk of bread, offered me half of it. The river was still covered with a white carapace, above it the clouds were beginning to turn pale. He ate, then became still, silent, his gaze directed beyond the river. I looked at him attentively, insistently even. '. . . Those who have no one to pray for them,' I thought again.

'So, d'you want to go and see her?' he said suddenly, without looking at me.

'See who?' I asked, perplexed.

'Don't play silly buggers. You know very well. That nurse.'

'Why should I? You're mad.'

He said nothing, his eyes once more lost among the bushes along the riverbanks. Frantically I racked my brains over what it was in our talks together that had betrayed me. Nothing. And everything . . . Every word, every gesture.

'Give me your hand,' he said in almost brutal tones, and got up. I held out my right hand, he pushed it away, seized my other hand and, before I could react, slashed the palm with a lump of ice, or so it seemed to me. No, it was a five-kopeck piece, sharpened into a razor-blade. The shallow cut glistened, began to bleed.

'You can tell her it was that rusty binload of shit . . .' I stood there, irresolute, looking now at him, now at the thread of blood. 'Go on,' he said more softly, without brutality, and he gave me a kindly smile, such as I had never seen on any face at the orphanage.

At the sick bay I was plunged for several minutes in that hypnotic state the woman's slowness generated around her. A blissful state for me, a blend of maternal gentleness and loving tenderness.

Nothing now remained of Samoylov's collection of books in the sealed-off room other than volumes badly damaged by the fire. My hands covered in ash, I was trying to resuscitate them, chiefly out of respect for their infirm state. Often reading became impossible. I would just have time to focus on a page scorched by the fire and already it was disintegrating in my fingers, carrying away its contents for ever. Thus it was that I read, without being able to re-read, a short poem in which the scenes depicted were strangely in harmony with the fragility of this single reading. I did not know the author, doubtless one of the obscure poets on the fringes of the Romantic movement. Samoylov's library, assembled with the omnivorous appetite of a neophyte, was well stocked with these names neglected by the anthologies and might well, I would tell myself years later, have formed the basis for an original history of literature, almost in parallel with the one that is taught and honoured.

The poem had as its title 'The Last Square', probably borrowed from Victor Hugo, echoing the warlike epics of the early nineteenth century. The soldiers formed up in this square were falling one by one, under attack from a more numerous and better armed enemy. The hero expressed only one fear, that of seeing his companions weaken. They stood firm, however (a couplet would come back to me one day in which *batterie* – the battery – rhymed with *fratrie* – brotherhood), closing ranks in the square to fill the gaps left by the dead. At the end only two were left, the hero and his friend. Back to back they fought on, out of pure gallantry, each one fearing to leave the other on his own. When finally the warrior's heart was pierced he looked round and in his friend's place he saw an angel, whose powerful wings were flecked with blood.

The page crumbled between my fingers like a fine sliver of slate. This ephemeral aspect reinforced the impact of the words. Few lines of verse have remained so vividly in my memory as these unknown stanzas.

\*      \*      \*

I remember, too, one of the last times (perhaps the very last) I spent reading in Alexandra's company. That evening at the end of March it stayed light for a long time; we could drink our tea and read without lighting the lamps. Sometimes a train would go by and in its lit compartments the lives of the passengers could be covertly observed: a woman tucking in a sheet on her couchette, a young man, his hands held up like blinkers, his brow pressed against the window, as if he hoped to see those he had just left behind . . . Alexandra had opened the window, the mild air brought in with it the pleasantly bitter scent of the last mounds of snow, the swollen bark of the trees. Promise of spring. I thought of this as I observed Alexandra reading aloud, the ghost of a smile playing over her lips. For the first time I thought about what a woman could feel at the coming of a new spring. A woman of her age. Or perhaps age did not count?

The book she was reading came from the devastated library, the accumulation of volumes by forgotten authors that had included 'The Last Square'. This one was a collection of short tales, interesting only for their elegant construction, maintaining the suspense for the space of half a page before the final triumph of Good. I was listening, lulled by all these predictable happy endings, when the next story, even shorter than the others, suddenly upset all these neat narrative rhythms. A young man falls passionately in love with a young woman, as cruel as she is beautiful, he declares his love to her and offers her his heart. 'No, my dear, I already have your heart. To prove to me that you love me truly, bring me your mother's heart. Yes, rip the heart out from her breast.' The lover runs home, stabs his mother, makes off with her heart. In his haste to satisfy his beloved, he stumbles on the journey, falls and drops the heart, which lands among stones. The lover groans, gets up and suddenly hears an anxious voice, his mother's heart speaking: 'You're not hurt, are you, my son?'

I had no memory of getting to my feet, leaving the room, running. Quite simply, after a total loss of awareness, I found myself standing in the sealed-off room, to which I had gained access by going out onto the landing, sliding along against the wall of the house on an old skirting-board and pushing open the door. There I was, biting my lip until it bled, so as not to howl, my eyes seeing nothing at first, then seeing the space outside the door: the fields blanketed with tired grey snow, the sky dull, spring. A world at once perfectly familiar and unrecognizable. Alexandra did not call me, she left me alone, waited quietly for me to come down. And never referred to that story again.

Many years later the difference between one's mother tongue and an acquired language was to become a fashionable topic. I would often hear it said that only the former could evoke the deepest and most subtle – the most untranslatable – ties that bind our souls. Then I would think of maternal love, which I had first discovered and experienced in French, in a quite simple little book, its pages tarnished by the fire.

Under the sun's blaze, immense slabs of ice slid down the river, collided, broke up, revealing their greenish rims, sometimes several feet thick. Just as we were crossing over the bridge a section of floating ice struck one of the pillars. The roadway shook beneath our feet. The impact made an explosion of sound. Breaking ranks, we rushed over to the handrail. It was giddy intoxication: the dazzle of the shafts of light, the wild chill of the liberated waters, the brutish power of the ice floes, rearing against the pillar, jolting upwards in spasms. On the opposite bank, looking like black ants, children played at rafting, leaping from one slab of floating ice to the next. As the white surface broke up, the young daredevils would dash onto the broadest fragment, which in its turn disintegrated, now driving them back onto terra firma, now, for the wildest of them, onto a slab whose instability demanded the contortions of a tightrope walker. Seen from the eminence of the bridge, these games were reminiscent of the flickering of a kaleidoscope.

During those spring months our own life, too, was reminiscent of a kaleidoscope, where the tube has been shattered so that, bit by bit, the glass sequins and mirrors spill out. Events followed one another, not so much leading us on to the future as draining our years in the orphanage, down to the last fragment of a dream.

During the course of a few weeks several people ran

away, really ran away, never to return, one of them ending up, so we learned, in the Far East. Then just before the May celebrations one of the girls was escorted by the director into an ambulance parked near the entrance. It was difficult to grasp that an adolescent of fourteen, a thin girl with drab features, was about to become a mother, and that since the previous autumn she had been carrying this other life within her and contrived not to give herself away in our midst, as we scribbled on the pages of our textbooks and told jokes about Brezhnev.

On one of the first evenings of May it became clear to me that the world of other people was going to exact a tribute from us. I was leaning against a tall table beside a kiosk where they served beer. I had no money but, as long as the serving woman did not notice my presence, I could listen to the customers' conversations. They were almost all men who, before returning joylessly to their homes (I was discovering that a family home could be joyless), were here flaunting their virility, discussing women (two categories: those who 'did it' and the rest), cursing the injustice of fate. There were not many women in this male preserve. Only one that evening, two tables away from mine. The man with her was addressing her in tones of such contempt that it was as if at every word he was gathering up his saliva to spit. At one moment he struck her with a dry, furtive little slap. She turned her face away, I recognized her. It was Muza, a girl from the orphanage, three years older than myself. She may have had some Caucasian or Tatar blood in her veins for her features were remarkably finely formed, one of those faces whose nobility and harmony make one doubt the animal origins of the human race. No one amongst the pupils at the orphanage had ever ventured to court her. For us, such a degree of beauty placed her in another living species, somewhere between a snow-laden branch and a shooting star . . .

There were not many customers, the booth was about to close. I could clearly hear the words the man was hissing through his teeth: 'You'll go just where I tell you, you dirty little whore . . . If it weren't for me you'd not even have anything to cover your arse with . . .' Muza shook her head in protest. At this, with a hate-filled grimace, the man very calmly pinched her lower lip, thrusting his finger into her now distorted mouth. He was twice her age and his beige suit and the colour of his sparse hair made him look like a long cigar with the tobacco spilling out of it. She tried to break free but he squeezed her mouth more violently, preventing her from speaking. With his thumb thrust in behind her cheek she managed to mumble in pitifully comic tones: 'I know where to go, I do. I shan't sleep in the street . . .' He released his grip, sneering as if disgusted: 'Oh yes. Go back to your filthy hole. They'll soon be kicking you all out . . .' She began to weep and I was struck by these tears, for she sobbed like a woman already mature, already wearied by life.

The waitress made half a dozen empty tankards clink as she picked them up with fanned-out fingers. 'All right, you. You'd better finish your lollipop or I'll call the militiaman. He's not far away. Hop it, before I get angry!'

I walked away regretting that I had not intervened, with that feeling of shame every man experiences a dozen or more times in his life. This particular time would remain one of the most painful for me.

I was not alone in having seen Muza in the company of the man who looked like a beige cigar. Some days later one of the boys claimed to have spied on them in a boat moored upstream from the orphanage. Despite the salacious exaggerations in his story I believed him, for the behaviour of the beige man, as he described it, corresponded precisely to what I had seen. Stuttering with excitement, he described the man seated in the boat, his trousers unbuttoned, his lower abdomen exposed, whistling to himself, while Muza, on her knees, had her head pressed against his stomach, although her hair made it impossible to see anything . . . Proud of his success, the storyteller went over the scene once more, described how the man stared at the clouds and whistled to himself, while the woman's mouth was distorted by the strenuous thrusting. . . . Village, who never took part in our discussions, suddenly broke into our circle and, without saying anything, struck. The storyteller collapsed, his arms flailing, got up, his lips bloody, hurled an oath and fell silent as he met Village's look. A look not threatening but sad.

In one other way or another we all approved of what Village had done, even the one who had received the blow.

I saw the nurse again in May on a public holiday. She was coming out of a shop, holding one handle of a huge shopping bag. The other handle was held by . . . I thought at first: her twin brother. But it was her husband and he looked like a comical masculine copy of her. Almost the same height, middling. The same build, rather well rounded. Fair, diaphanous curls, the man's even more dazzling. I experienced neither jealousy nor disappointment. The couple looked like little piglets in a strip cartoon and could therefore have nothing in common with the silent woman who had tended my wound. With all my strength I wanted to believe in the possibility that this was her double. Within the cracked kaleidoscope of our lives I at least needed this shard of a dream to hold onto.

Among the flickering reflected visions there were also those two girls and their boyfriends, chatting at the entrance to a lane. We saw them from a lorry bringing us back from a work site. The driver had parked it under the trees and had gone off in search of a packet of cigarettes. One of the boys was seated on his bicycle, the other was holding his by the handlebars. Fenced in, as we were, by the sides of the lorry, we studied them in their little carefree oasis. Their freedom enthralled us. Even their skin was different from ours. After several baking hot days our faces were peeling, our short hair was rough and discoloured. The golden skin of these girls gave evidence of a mysterious way of life in which one took care of one's body, as of an asset . . . At one moment the boy seated on his bike took hold of a fine lock of hair that had slipped over his girlfriend's cheek and tucked it back behind her ear. She seemed not to notice this action, continued talking. I sensed around me a swift muscular tension, like there is at the cinema, when the hero draws closer to danger . . . A volley of oaths erupted in the midst of our tightly-packed crowd. Laughter, obscenities, banging on the metal of the cabin and then, as if someone had given the order for it, silence. The two couples moved off rapidly down the lane beneath the trees. A girl leaning on the panel beside me had her eyes swollen with tears.

*     *     *

74

From the same broken kaleidoscope this spray of sparks came fizzing out: the town hooligans, who sometimes arrived to taunt us, were armed with short, double-edged weapons known as 'Finnish knives'. On that particular evening the impact of a blade against an iron bar in the already darkening air caused a tiny spurt of blue-green. We had yet to discover that these brawls were, in fact, a means for the local underworld to test our mettle. For it was from among youths such as ourselves that they recruited people with nothing to lose and no one to love. This burst of sparks fixed in my vision the flat, ugly face of one of our assailants. Some days later I was to pass him near the station. He was giving the beige man a light.

It was from this station that I used to set out for the township where Alexandra lived. I had not been back to see her since the May celebrations and it was already the end of the month. The passengers were talking about a fire that had just destroyed a railway depot, the warm breeze carried a bitter taste of charred resin . . . Not finding Alexandra at home, I went downstairs, walked round the house and caught sight of her in the distance, standing beside the tracks. I saw her from behind but guessed at her gesture: her hand shading her eyes, she was looking up at the clouds of smoke above the long buildings of the depot. The train traffic had been interrupted, the firemen's helmets were glinting amid the rails. You could hear the crash of beams collapsing, the hiss of fire hoses. From time to time the murk framed a ghostly sun through the smoke, and the day froze into the contrasting black and white of a negative. Then the vividness of the flames and the intensity of the sky would flood back into this momentary dusk. The clusters of flowers on a lilac bush next to a buffer between the tracks seemed to be blooming on another day in another world.

Alexandra looked a tiny figure beside the soaring clouds of smoke, against the horizon of the plain towards which the empty tracks led. I stared at her and, more clearly than ever, believed I understood who she was. I recalled how her neighbour, the old Tatar, Yussuf, had once remarked to her: 'You know Alexandra, you Russians . . .' He was right, this woman standing amid the railway lines, her gaze fixed on the flames, was Russian. Time had erased in her everything that could still distinguish her from the life of this country, its wars, its sorrows, its sky. She was as much a part of it as the quivering of a blade of grass amid the endless ocean swell of the steppe. She had invented a remote homeland and a language for herself. But her real homeland was that tiny room in an old wooden house, half destroyed by bombs. That house and the infinity of the steppes all around. The place where she would remain forever incarcerated, the prisoner of an era made up of wars and suffering. I felt myself reeling on the brink of this past, in danger of letting myself be drawn into its yawning darkness. I must distance myself from it, flee.

A ball of fire, fringed with soot, billowed up over the depot. Alarmed, I drew back, and focused an uneasy gaze once more upon the figure of Alexandra, who was still there, unmoving. And I made off very quickly, jumping over the sleepers. I was afraid I might see her turning, calling me . . .

In the train I thought about the language she had taught me. Its words, I knew, had no bearing on anything in the world that surrounded us. I remembered Muza and her beauty, the beige man, the story told by the boy who had spied on them . . . One of the last poems I had come across in the ruins of Samoylov's library spoke of a pair of lovers disporting themselves in 'a meadow shimmering with a thousand flowers'. I suddenly felt something akin to disgust for the affectation of this torrent of words. Outside the carriage window the monotony of the steppe unfolded, dry and rough, stained blood-red by the sunset.

So what I had learned was a dead language.

On my return to the orphanage I noticed that Village was absent, he had not come in to supper. I caught up with him amid the willow groves on the riverbank at one of his fishing spots. He was embarrassed to be discovered constructing a child's toy: a tiny raft made of sticks that he was binding together with strips of bark. The remains of a fire were smouldering gently. So as not to lose face, he explained to me with a wink: 'Look at this. First off, it's going to float down our river. Then, whoosh, onto the Volga. And then, as long as a pike doesn't have it for breakfast, straight onto the Caspian Sea. One day those Persians'll be picking it up, you mark my words!' Using a piece of wood, he lifted several still-glowing brands out of the embers, laid them on his raft and put it in the water. We stayed there for a long while, watching these tiny lights as they drifted away in the purple air of the dusk.

On the footpath that led back up to the orphanage he confided to me in somewhat embarrassed tones: 'You know that boat where that bastard and Muza . . . Well . . . I've sunk it now . . .'

*     *     *

Twenty years later, when I was beginning to write, I contemplated turning that evening spent in the company of Village into a short story about the last twenty-four hours in the life of a young man. For he was to die at the end of the following day. A striking subject, I thought, the quintessence of a life revealed amid the mellow banality of a May dusk. I never wrote it, no doubt sensing the falseness of a contrivance of this kind. Instead of reinventing those twenty-four hours in such a way as to milk them for significance, I needed to hold on to what little I knew of them, and tell it, while avoiding the temptation to wax philosophical.

The following evening (it was a Sunday) the same gang of loutish 'recruiting sergeants' appeared and this time invited us out for a drink. It was clear that – between the stick and the carrot – they were seeking out our weak spots. We did not refuse, some of our number eager to act like hard men and others, perhaps all of us, eager to respond to the least promise of friendship. They drank, too, and had probably not even foreseen the brawl that erupted on account of an overturned glass, an oath, a slap. Or else, on the contrary, everything was calculated, to divide us up into those who would nibble the carrot and those who would resist.

The only weapons we had were our five-kopeck pieces sharpened into blades, then an iron bar snatched from one of the louts, a broken bottle . . . I already knew that hand-to-hand combat only looked good in films and that this brawl would be much like the previous ones: clumsy shuffling, blows missing the target, no mercy for those that fell, animal glee at any sign of weakness. The alcohol made the fight even uglier, we all simply felt we were saving our own skins. One of our number was already on the ground, huddled in on himself like a scarab, to ward off blows to his head.

I noticed Village during a moment's respite as, with broken bottle in hand, I contrived to keep at bay an adversary as out of breath as I was. Village was coming up from the river, doubtless attracted by our gasps and groans. I saw him drop his lines, pick up a big stone, rush towards us. Then a few minutes later (finding I had time to spit out a fragment of broken tooth) I saw him again. Inexplicably the assault by the louts had just started to falter, they were retreating, one of them, tapping the others on the back, was urging them to leave. At length they all ran across a patch of waste ground, leaving us an unhoped-for victory. Now we were laughing, wiping away the blood, discussing the best bits of the fight . . . Suddenly we heard this voice. We saw Village sitting there, his arms lolling on the ground and, as it seemed to us, glassy-eyed with astonishment. He was not groaning but from his lips came forth a wet babbling, like that of a babe-in-arms. Someone touched his shoulder, Village toppled gently backwards. We gathered round him, crouching, made uneasy by this fixed stare, clumsily felt his chest, his head . . . All the arms clutching at him seemed to be straining to hold him back on a slippery slope. There was still time for one of our number to jokingly suggest a glass of vodka, but already beneath the unbuttoned shirt a fine trickle of blood was to be seen and the grey glint of a blade – that of a 'Finnish knife', which had snapped at the hilt.

All I can remember of our headlong run to the orphanage and the minutes that followed it is the desperate hammering on the sick-bay door: we had forgotten it was a Sunday.

During the days that followed I was haunted by the notion that this death demanded some gesture from me, some idea I could not succeed in coming up with. Some serious, significant gesture. But the trifling nature of everything that happened was distressing to me. The next day, just as if nothing had occurred, the nurse opened the sick bay at nine o'clock precisely. Two days later they ordered us to carry out our old desks from the classrooms and among the table tops covered in drawings and writing, nobody took note of the one that had belonged to Village. Trifling, too, was my feverish speculation about the odds: if only I had thought of taking along the *Misericordia* dagger that day, then, perhaps . . . Yet I knew a blow from an iron bar would have smashed that slender blade like glass.

Then, one evening at the beginning of June, I found a way to force myself from this verbiage of remorse as I remembered the little raft Village had launched on its nocturnal voyage. It suddenly seemed to me that it was very important to keep picturing this tiny craft with its freight of smoky charcoal. Not to allow its slow progress towards the Caspian Sea to be interrupted in my mind. To believe it was still afloat.

At the time of the funeral we had all noted that there was no one to inform about Village's death. For us this was not a new idea, but we were struck by the cosmic absoluteness of it: no one upon the whole terrestrial globe! That priest's words, heard during the preceding winter, came back to me then: '. . . Those who have no one to pray for them.' Once more I pictured the little raft, the glowing embers drifting away into the night beneath the Volga's immense sky.

# Four

The sky white with heat, the timeless lethargy of the steppes, a bird flapping its wings, unable to progress in the extreme density of the void. Like the bird, we moved forwards with no other points of reference than the remoteness of the plains and a horizon made molten by the flow of overheated air. The gigantic excavator advancing in front of us ripped open the earth's crust with its bucket wheel, tracing an endless straight line. Covered in dust, deafened by the roar of the machine and the grinding of crushed rocks, we dragged along lengthy slabs of pine which the workmen used to reinforce the sides of this future irrigation canal. As if in the mad hope of containing the changeless surge of the infinite with this ephemeral casing . . . In the evening our weariness could be gauged by the buzzing of a bee beating against the walls of the barrack hut, which no one had the strength left to chase away. That would have meant getting up, stepping over bodies stretched out on their bunks, flapping a shirt, steering the insect towards the door . . . But we were already asleep and its hum became the start of our dreams.

To melt into this desert of light was the best way to forget, the best way to mourn, the best way to forget mourning. We talked a good deal less than in previous years, when we had still viewed this summertime penal servitude as a purgatory with promise. Now we knew that the future would not be very different from this daily trudge of ours behind the disembowelling machine, from the absurdly stubborn line of this ditch, whose sides must be unremittingly strengthened.

One day, along with scoops of earth, the excavator began hurling out human remains, skulls, soldiers' boots, helmets from the last war. On another occasion there were much older bones, ancient helms, swords brown with rust . . . a millennium may well have separated these warriors from the others. A thousand years of sleep. Ten centuries of nothingness. The next day when the machine ploughed on, away from these ransacked graves, we saw archaeologists moving into the area. A handful of black specks lost amid the sunlit void of the plain.

As in previous summers, our work was often interrupted: they would disguise us in white short-sleeved shirts and clean trousers and take us to appear as extras on vast esplanades, where important visitors were making speeches in front of commemorative monuments and concrete obelisks. In this way we were privileged one day to see a certain North Korean leader, from a distance as always. He spent a long time reading from a sheaf of papers which the warm breeze, very strong that day, threatened to snatch away from him at every moment. This man, who was puny and had a slight stoop, was battling to control the flapping sheets like a seaman unable to master a shivering sail . . . There was also an African statesman, who decided to hold forth in Russian and spoke very slowly, detaching each syllable from the next and getting the stresses all wrong. The tip of the monument showed greenish-white against a dark, storm-laden sky. The lazy rumble of thunder beyond the river sounded like muffled laughter someone was trying to repress. But we did not flinch: the photographers needed us in unmoving ranks, with faces all turned in the same direction . . . Many years later, whenever I came across my former comrades, we would regret not having paid more attention to all those VIP guests. As time went by we would have been able to identify them, some still active in political life, some having passed into the pages of history books. But in those days we were simply waiting for the moment when our patience would be rewarded with a dip in the Volga. That summer, however, even these bathes did not spark off the raucous enthusiasm of the old days.

The narrow fanlight in our barrack hut was broken and every evening before we went to sleep we would see a beautiful rainbow of light spawned by the crack in the glass, a long peacock's tail suddenly flooding the cluttered interior of our dwelling for a few minutes, slipping along towards the nails where our earth-stained clothes hung. One evening this solar spectrum did not materialize. We were at the end of June, the angle of the sun's rays had changed. Nobody said anything, but I frequently saw glances straying towards our 'cloakroom', now left in shadow. Having been completely forgetful of time, that salutary forgetfulness the steppe bestowed on us, we were suddenly remembering that this was the last summer we should spend together.

The next morning, close beside the line of the canal, we came upon a wooden cross with a helmet hanging from one of its arms. We gathered round it, intrigued by the anonymity and loneliness of this tomb amid the immensity of the plains blinded by the sun. What we were used to seeing was mountains of concrete celebrating death, gilded inscriptions, effigies of heroes. Here, just two lengths of birchwood with cracked bark, a mound long since levelled off by the winds. Strangely enough, the sight of this tomb provoked no distress, offered no invitation to share pain. There was even something light and ethereal, almost carefree, about the cross. Its presence at this spot (why just here and not two hundred miles to the north or south?), the human randomness of its presence, seemed to indicate that what really mattered was taking place somewhere other than beneath this rectangle of earth . . .

From the far side of the channel a supervisor called out to us: 'Look lively! We're off now! There's a ceremony . . .' It was the hallowed formula for our work as extras.

It got off to a bad start this time. We took five hours to reach the site and, disguised as Pioneers bold and true in our red neckerchiefs, we began to wait, cooped up in the bus at the side of a road. Evidently they were not certain whether they would need us or not. In the old days we would have hatched a rebellion, demanded bread, simulated a collective attack of diarrhoea. That day each of us remained alone with his thoughts, some trying to sleep, others taking refuge in the memory of a special day, a special smile. The supervisors seemed more than usually on edge. Yet, according to the rumours, all that was involved was the visit of a general. And we had seen field marshals, even a cosmonaut . . .

An official in a dark suit suddenly climbed onto the steps of the coach and uttered a kind of whispered shout:

'Quick! Get out! They're coming. Quick! Get fell in!' He had a red face, seemed panic-struck.

They led us at the double onto a broad terrain at the top of a hill, which was already surrounded by several detachments of young extras. One corner of this living frame appeared to be empty; they filled the breach with our troops. Once we were installed there I glanced behind us. In the distance the empty window frames of a half-finished building were clearly visible. So we were there to hide it from the visitors . . . What we had to do now, as we all knew from past experience, was to sink as rapidly as possible into a torpid state that would make us impervious to the burning heat of the sun, thirst and the absurd duration of the ceremony. To concentrate on the shape of a cloud that was gradually, very gradually, growing longer . . .

Suddenly a swift tensing of muscles around me jerked me out of my drowsy state. Thanks to our communal existence, we had synchronized reflexes. I brought my eyes into focus, observed the esplanade. A crowd of notabilities, doubtless the town's administrators, was already present, looking towards the other end of the space, where there was a break in the surrounding line of white shirts, leaving a broad way in. All my comrades' eyes were fixed on this opening. Quite a large group of people was approaching at a steady pace, as always happened in ceremonies of this kind; so far there was nothing extraordinary about this procession . . .

All at once I saw what was extraordinary.

My first impression was the most unlikely and yet the most accurate: 'The Lilliputians leading the captured Gulliver . . .' The man walking at the centre of the group was at least a head taller than all the others. Or rather, his head and shoulders were visible above the bobbing motion of the faces surrounding him. I looked for the glint of a general's gold braid, a cap with the kind of insignia I imagined from the generals' uniforms in our army. But the giant who was at the heart of the ceremony from the very first moment wore a dark suit devoid of any hint of rank. Perhaps only in his gait, in his rather stiff way of planting his feet on the ground, in the firm carriage of his body, was there something military about him. Moreover, as he drew closer I perceived that it was not his exceptional height that gave him his central position but his way of shaping the space around him.

I could already see his face, with an expression reminiscent of a wise and disenchanted old elephant, and his eyelids that lifted slowly to reveal a penetrating gaze of surprising vitality. Very close to me I suddenly heard someone murmur with admiring apprehension: 'Did you see the nose on him?' This powerful eminence was a source of fascination in the land of the steppes, where the flat faces of Asia prevailed. But the enthusiastic whisper in fact signified something else: the arrival of such a man was bound to cause something of a sensation.

And the sensation was forthcoming. A man with a *kolkhoz* director's banal features emerged from the group of town notabilities and walked towards the old giant, who had stopped with his entourage in the middle of the space. Although we were standing to attention I had a sense of a slight creaking of vertebrae: all necks were being craned towards an incredible spectacle.

For the director of the *kolkhoz*, or the man who looked like one, was carrying an enormous sturgeon, holding it by its gills. It looked rather as if he were dancing with the monstrous fish, whose mouth was poking into his face and whose tail was trying to wrap itself round the calves of his legs. The creature's weight compelled the dancer to lean his body backwards and walk with jerky steps, as if in a strange, swaying tango. He was already drawing close to the giant. Everyone held their breath.

When they were a few paces apart an optical illusion occurred. The sturgeon began to shrink, to seem less long, less heavy. Finally, when the gift took its place in the guest's hands, the silvery body of the fish seemed almost slender. It was displayed to the audience as a fine fishing trophy, held aloft without apparent effort. The beaming giant's strength was applauded. Then a top administrator, all the way from Moscow, stepped up to the microphone and began speaking, his eyes fixed on the typewritten sheets.

I saw neither the speaker nor the crowd of notabilities. I had just solved the true mystery of the tall old man. At that moment, having entrusted the fish to one of his aides, he had taken advantage of the noise of the ovation and with a conjuror's dexterity – all the while approving with his head the words his entourage were addressing to him, and which he was not listening to – he had slipped his right hand into his jacket pocket, taken out a handkerchief and rapidly wiped his fingertips, which were no doubt sticky from the sturgeon's slime. I was possibly the only person to have observed his action and this detail, once noted, gave me the feeling that I had discovered his secret: it was his solitude. He was surrounded, acclaimed, lent himself with a good grace to all these diplomatic games, he even accepted the slimy monster and knew instinctively for how many seconds he should display the gift before handing it to his aide-de-camp. He was utterly present. And yet very much apart, in a profound, pensive solitude.

Now he was listening to the speech, with one ear cocked towards the interpreter, who had to stand on tiptoe. The more pompous the words became the more remote was his expression. At intervals a look flashed out from beneath his heavy eyelids. Like a tracer bullet it would target the crowd of notabilities, reach the ranks of the white shirts, land upon the speaker. At one moment his eyes rested on our square, and his eyebrows went up slightly, as if speculating about something that he would like to have had confirmed. But already the speaker was folding up his papers to the sound of obedient applause from the audience. With a measured tread, his head bowed in a gesture of concentration, the old giant made his way towards the microphone, which a technician hastily adjusted upwards. He produced no sheet of paper and among the Party officials there was a little flutter of anxiety: words spoken off the cuff were by their very nature subversive.

He spoke. And I was certain I was the only one who understood the language he gave voice to. It was the one I had believed dead. French.

The impression I had of being his only audience was not, by and large, false. The notabilities were incapable of listening to speeches not written down. The giant's entourage thought they knew in advance what was going to be said. The young extras with their red neckerchiefs were aware of the fine, powerful, occasionally somewhat strident music of his sentences but not of their meaning. The interpreters were concentrating on the syntax.

He said what had to be said at such a ceremony, in the ponderous presence of a concrete monument upon soil heavy with steel and the mortal remains of fighting men. But now, initiated into his secret, I believed I could hear a silent voice, hidden behind the ringing tones of his speech. He spoke of thousands of heroes, but the hidden voice brought to mind not these nameless, faceless thousands but the one who, perhaps, lay beneath our feet. He spoke of the gratitude of peoples, but a perceptible bitterness made it possible to sense that he knew how ungrateful a people can reveal itself to be towards those who have laid down their lives for it . . .

At one moment there was a brief stirring among his entourage. A mouth whispering in an ear, a discreet glance at a watch . . . The diplomats had no doubt noticed that things were running behind schedule for the visit. Like a hardened orator, the giant ignored this distraction, merely turning his head a little in the direction of their confabulations, with one eyebrow arched, as if to say: 'Silence in the ranks!' The sight of these people in their elegant suits irritated him. The rhythm of his words did not change. But his silent voice suddenly became still more audible to me, perceptible even as he spoke. 'Look at them, these bureaucrats! Already counting the time until the banquet. But do they know how much time it took a company to secure this hill? And how many lives it cost to hold it? Do you know how many eternities each second lasts as you force yourself up from the ground and run out under fire?'

Suddenly he fell silent. Someone thought the speech was finished. Two or three hesitant handclaps rang out. Then everyone froze, their eyes riveted to this man in the middle of the space. His stillness turned him into a tall monolith, indifferent to human emotion. Amid this silence, that had fallen from the sky, or so it seemed to us, the mighty blast of the hot wind could be heard, sweeping across the plain.

For several moments the old giant directed his gaze into the distance, over our heads, beyond the unfinished building they had sought to hide from him, beyond the Volga, into the endless solitude of the steppes. And I believed he could even see the cross made from two branches of birchwood, above an unknown grave.

This minute of silence (in reality six or seven seconds) was very likely involuntary but it altered the whole sense of the ceremony. The giant roused himself and in a final coda, yet more throaty than his earlier words, he spoke of victory, of honour, of the mother country. He raised his arms and our hearts went with them. The applause, perhaps for the first time ever at such a ceremony, was sincere.

The officials surrounded him, re-forming their Lilliputian escort, and began guiding him towards the downward slope. But, with his art of making space pliant to his will, he broke through their circle and walked with giant strides along the line formed by the young. The extras in their white shirts smiled broadly, each one waved the carnation he had been issued with for the occasion. The giant passed by, eyeing them with just a tinge of disappointment. In front of our square he halted. We had no flowers, we were not smiling, remained at attention. I do not know if he grasped who we were, with our peeling faces and cropped hair, and the minimal difference between boys and girls. I think he did. He must, at all events, have realized that we came from another era, the era they were trying to bury beneath the concrete of the memorial. The era that was dear to him. He looked at us, nodded his head and screwed up his eyes, as if to say: 'Chin up!' And we saw him walking away, not with his entourage, but with an elderly army officer. The two of them had no need of the interpreter weaving his way between them. The military man was making broad gestures, no doubt explaining troop movements, the deployment of artillery pieces, breakthroughs of armoured divisions. The old giant approved, making up with his hands for the hesitations of the interpreter, now trailing behind . . .

I spoke to the supervisor, who was waiting for us beside the bus, in the manner of a condemned man formulating his last request: 'There's someone in the city I must see. My aunt . . . If I'm not allowed to go, I'll run away all the same.' He gave me a searching look, gauging the unstable frontier between the unlimited submissiveness we normally displayed and a rebellion that might erupt at the most unexpected moment. At that very moment indeed, just as we were being promised a whole morning of bathing in the Volga the following day. As a good psychologist, he sensed that here was an exceptional case. 'If you don't show up tomorrow I'll set the militia on you as a fugitive. It'll be a re-education colony for you. Don't say I didn't warn you. Now, hop it. You can still catch the last train. Hang on: take this as your ticket.'

The following morning Alexandra telephoned him and, on the pretext of sunstroke and a high fever, won for me the handful of days I was to spend with her that came to count for more in my life than some whole years.

I had arrived at about ten o'clock at night and, without explaining anything, told her everything in such breathless haste that it could indeed have been taken for fever or the early stages of drunkenness. The window overlooking the railway tracks was open, you could hear the heavy clanking of a train on its way from the Urals. She made tea, lit the lamp. It was only when she asked in a very calm voice, too calm: 'So what did he speak about?' that I sensed her emotion.

I took a deep breath and suddenly felt utterly tongue-tied. I could tell her about the handkerchief wiping away the slime from the sturgeon. I recalled the smallest of the giant's gestures. I even had a memory of the moment when he used the past historic tense of a verb that sounded old fashioned to my ear (some '*naquit*' or quite simply '*fut*') that had struck me like the sighting of a prehistoric reptile. I could easily have said: 'He spoke about the war and the victory and the debt all peoples owe to their heroes . . .' But the real essence of it was not there. It was in that silent voice I believed I had heard, in the gaze he directed towards the forgotten cross in the middle of the plain . . . Yet how to speak of that? And indeed, was it real or had I dreamed it?

Seeing my confusion, Alexandra thought I had been

unable to follow the spoken French or that the content of the speech was too complex for a boy of my age. It was doubtless in order to rescue me from my predicament that, in tones of a very distant reminiscence, she said: 'He came here to the city once before. In forty-four. Yes, in the autumn of forty-four. I didn't see him. The hospital was full to bursting. Everyone was working day and night. But we had already talked about him for the first time long before that . . .'

'Who is "we"?' I asked, emerging from my torpor.

' "We" is myself and . . . Jacques Dorme.'

My 'sunstroke' lasted for less than a week. But Jacques Dorme's life story, the fragmentary sketch of this life story, had time to knit itself for ever into what I was. The tale Alexandra told me that July 1966 was one of those you hear only once in a lifetime.

Four years and a few months after that ceremony on the esplanade, I learned of the tall old man's death. The gaze that embraced the steppe beyond the Volga, the moment of silence he had spun out that day, all this had just vanished into eternity. I can still see the newspaper kiosk near the Anichkov Bridge in Leningrad, the page with his picture on it, the report of his death. 'The Lilliputians have won,' I thought, as I bought the paper. I could not yet guess how accurate this phrase was. But I was already grown up enough to know that prior to this death there had been betrayal by some, cowardice by others. Above all the ingratitude of a country, whose honour he had once saved.

In my memory, however, he would remain unchanged: an old giant in the middle of a former battlefield, paying homage to fallen warriors. Just one sentence of his, which I was to come across much later in a book, would be added to this vision of him, as if in reply to Alexandra's question as to what he had spoken about: 'Now that baseness is in the ascendant it is they who can look upon Heaven without turning pale and upon Earth without blushing.'

# Five

On that day any distance between the painful duty of living and the calm acceptance of death vanishes.

A day in May 1942, some twenty miles from Stalingrad, the heat as dense as tar, the railway tracks littered with dirty bandages, fragments of bombs, rubbish. A train has been hit. The railwaymen are trying to disconnect the tank wagon that is on fire so as to shunt it onto a siding. As the oil in it blazes, it plunges the surrounding area into a night shot through by a purple sun. The other trains advance tentatively now, but do not come to a halt – the only thing that matters. Westbound trains: soldiers, shells, arms, armaments. Eastbound trains: mangled flesh, the residue of battles. The monstrous culinary process of war, an immense cauldron that has to be fed at every moment with tons of steel, oil, blood.

Alexandra finds herself caught between the wall of immobilized tank wagons and the line of coaches moving forwards on the neighbouring track. If the fire spreads, the rail junction will become an inferno over half a mile long. She ought to drop to the ground, crawl under the train, emerge the other side, escape. She does not stir, stares at her reflection in the tank wagon's side that glistens with oil. Mute. Suddenly her Christian name rings out within her, her real Christian name, and her

French surname. Her life, adrift here in this noonday twilight, in a foreign land that is in its death throes all about her. The brownish air, the cries of the wounded, her own body melting in the heat, stained, exhausted with her efforts, asphyxiated. She tells herself death could never sweep her away at a moment of greater anguish. At the end of the train the smoke grows thicker, the track is no longer visible . . .

Her reflection begins to slip away, disappears. They have managed to cut the train in two, and tow away the burning portion. Life can resume. A life that could so easily be mistaken for death.

Through the pounding of the wheels she hears a voice calling her: 'Shura!' She returns to her Russian life, gets back to work. Day after day, together with other women, she unravels the tangle of the trains, the comings and goings of the locomotives. It all happens amid the tension of raw nerves, in a mêlée of yelling and oaths, oblivious of tiredness, of hunger, of oneself. An engine driver swears at her, her fierce response is curt and effective. A colleague helps her to lift a dead man down from the train that carries the wounded. They take hold of him, set him down on a pile of old sleepers. The man's eyes are open, seem animated; you can see the smoke rising from the fire in them. Two more trains squeeze her between their walls, one travelling westwards (the plaintive sound of an accordion, the smiling face of a soldier who cups his hands and asks her to marry him), the other eastwards, silent (at a window a head entirely swathed in bandages, a mouth trying to snatch a little air). And for her, between these two moving walls, the illusion of solitude and repose. And this thought: why do I cling on to this hell? She studies her right hand, her fingers injured in an air-raid. Great soldier's boots on her feet. Without seeing it, she senses the withered and aged mask of her face.

The two trains clear at almost the same moment. A man comes walking along, stepping over the tracks, calmly swinging a little suitcase, careless of the chaotic manoeuvring of the trains. He is dressed in a bizarre outfit, part military, part civilian. His unfettered gait, the glances he throws all about him, make him look like someone taking a peaceful Sunday walk who has landed by chance in this day of war. For several seconds he remains hidden behind the coils of smoke, then reappears, dodges a locomotive by a hair's breadth, continues his stroll. 'A German spy . . .' Alexandra says to herself, mindful of the countless posters that call for the unmasking of these enemies, who are being dropped in by parachute behind the lines in vast numbers, or so it appears. Shielding his eyes, the man observes the rapid flight of a fighter plane above the flames, then heads towards the signal box. No, too clumsy for a spy. This one is going to end up under the wheels of a track trolley or of the train that now materializes, cleaving through the smoke. Alexandra starts running towards the man, signalling to him to move away, trying to make her cry heard above the grinding wheels on the track. She catches up with him, pushes him, they both stumble, lashed by the draught from the train. The words she hurls at him also hiss like lashes. Rough, coarse words that turn her voice into a man's voice. She knows the words are ugly, that she herself must be very ugly in the eyes of this errant holidaymaker, but she needs this revulsion, she seeks this pain, this inescapable torment. The stroller screws up his eyes, as if in an effort to understand, a smile on his lips. He replies, explaining calmly, with the incongruous politeness of another age. His speech is correct but this very correctness stands out. 'He's speaking with an accent,' she says to herself and suddenly, dumbfounded, incredulous, she thinks she has guessed what the accent is.

There is still time for them to exchange a few words in Russian but already the recognition is taking place, or rather a swift series of acts of recognition: the timbre of the voice, the body language, a gesture that a Russian would make differently. They start speaking French and she now feels as if it is she who speaks with an accent. After twenty years of silence in this language.

The same hell still surrounds them, the same restless labyrinth of trains, the same grating of steel, crushing the tiniest grain of silence on the track, the same aircraft propellers shredding the sky above their heads, and this smoke that throws the shadow of unknown days across their faces. They notice none of this. When the noise obliterates their voices they guess at words simply from the movement of lips. He gathers she is a nurse but was wounded three weeks ago and has been assigned to this signal box. She knows he mistook his direction at Stalingrad station and has so far failed to meet up with the squadron he has been posted to. But for the moment it is the sound of the words more than the meaning that matters, the simple possibility of recognizing them, of hearing these French words come to life. Of speaking the name of the town near Paris where she was born, that of another, his own home town, near Roubaix, in the north. Names that resonate, like passwords.

It will feel to them as if they have not been parted all day. At three o'clock in the morning they will still be talking, sitting in a room with no light, their tea cold in front of them. At a certain moment they will notice that the night has grown pale and daybreak has made its appearance through the shattered wall. They did, of course, go their separate ways after their encounter in the middle of the tracks: he to continue his search, she running towards the firemen's trolley. They had just enough time to arrange this rendezvous for very late in the evening. But from now on a different time exists for them, uninterrupted, invisible to other people, as fragile as the pallor slipping in through the hole in the wall, as the freshness of a wild cherry tree beneath the open window.

They should not have told one another the things they did tell, he, talking about the squadron he was to join (military secret!), she, admitting her fear (defeatism!): 'If the Germans cross the Volga the war is lost . . .' But they spoke in French, with the feeling that they were using a coded language, designed for confidences, one that took them far away from the smoke engulfing the railway tracks.

Particularly now, at around three in the morning, she takes stock of this remoteness. The first pallor in the sky, the scent of the wild cherry, a cool breeze blowing over from the Volga. The face of the man opposite her, the extra strong tea in their cups, tea he has brought with him, whose taste she had long since forgotten. Even the moments of silence between them are different from the silence she normally hears. Yet the inferno is very close, just a few hundred sleepers' distance from this house. By five o'clock she will be plunging back into it. The man will go and join his unit. She listens to him talking about the last days before the war, days he spent in Paris in August 1939. He was coming out of the cinema (he had just seen *Toute la Ville Danse* . . . 'Not bad . . . Nice music') when through an office window he saw this fair-haired woman rigged out in a gas mask, talking on the telephone. A training exercise . . . They laugh.

There is no order to the things they tell one another. They have too many years, too many faces to conjure up. In the darkness it costs her less pain to tell him about the grief she carries within her, which was choking her the previous day, when they met. Seven years before she had experienced the same desolation. Her husband ('My Russian husband . . .' she explains) had just been arrested and shot after a trial that lasted twenty minutes. At that time she had longed for death, had thought of death with a kind of gratitude, but had also pictured another solution: to escape from the Siberian town to which they had banished her and return to France. This idea had kept her alive. She had hunted down the slightest item of news from Paris. One day she had come upon a collection of texts: ten French writers translated into Russian. The first one was called: 'Stalin, the man who shows us the new world'. Then there was a poem that bore the title: 'Hymn to the GPU'. Lines in celebration of the secret police who had killed her husband, among millions of others . . . She had read the collection to the end – unable to picture what kind of human beings these Frenchmen could be, to picture the eyes that chose such ignoble blindness, the mouths that dared utter such words.

She tells Jacques Dorme that now this notion of getting back to France seems even more improbable than ever. Not on account of the French poets singing the GPU's praises but on account of the war, this one war that reaches from the Volga to the Seine. On account of all the trainloads of wounded, who must be sent to the rear.

He talks about the house where he spent his childhood and youth, the German units now marching down the street past the drawing-room windows. On the wall in this room there is a photo of his father, still very young, who went away to the war, the 'Great War', and came back from it an old man, to await his death in 1925. He does not know if the memory he retains of his father derives solely from this portrait or from the few seconds during which a three-year-old child sees a man on the front steps, with a knapsack slung across his shoulder, then the silhouette of this man walking away up the street and disappearing.

Next evening they are to meet again, once more with the feeling that they have not been parted from one another for a single moment.

'No pretender I. I am . . .'

Long years afterwards, when I thought about Jacques Dorme, it would be those words that best evoked for me the nature of the man, the unspoken credo of this pilot, this stranger who materialized amid the smoke from a blazing train. Words once uttered by a king of France.

In my youth I wanted to see him as a shining hero, his life as a series of glorious exploits. A habit of mind doubtless left over from our childish daydreams at the orphanage. But from the start of the story that Alexandra told me, my yearning for grand gestures was stilled by the simplicity of what I heard. A life that in no way sought to be moulded into a predestined course, one that lagged behind events and sometimes even came to a standstill, as it did during those nights spent in a room with one of its walls stove in, and open to the sky, admitting the tart fragrance of a wild cherry. Far away from the time-keeping of men.

He touched down in Spain too late (my desire to see him at the head of an international brigade proved to be vain). It was January 1939, two months after the fall of Madrid. Had he hoped to join the battle against Franco's air force and the German fighter planes, to fly a Dewoitine or a Potez, such as he had piloted in France? In any case the reality was different. He did not fight but retrieved the debris of lost battles: arms, the wounded, the dead. And he flew not a dashing fighter aircraft but a heavy three-engined transporter, a Junkers 52, captured from the Nazis.

He had certainly dreamed of aerial dogfights and little stars marked on the side of the cockpit, the tally of victories. But the suffering of crowds seeking refuge, the cunning multiplicity of sufferings devised by war, gave him a humbler notion of his pilot's task: it was to move people from a place of great suffering to a place where there would be less suffering.

He even ended up reconciling himself to his Boche aircraft. At first he had told himself that in the event of war with Germany, familiarity with it would be useful for knowing how best to shoot down planes of this type. In time the aircraft's patient reliability warmed their relationship into an almost human friendship, grudging but forgiving at critical moments. 'I have re-educated her,' he would say to the Russian pilots he often came across, who had taught him a smattering of their language. He could not yet guess at the importance these two details, insignificant in themselves, would one day assume: knowing this old Junkers aircraft and the ability to string together a dozen sentences in Russian.

Another thing he learned was that war memories tended to lie in ambush for a pilot, especially on the brink of sleep, where the skies they wove for him were cluttered with steel beams, fragments of cable and the branches of trees, through which his plane must steer a tortuous, unbearably slow course. He often woke up, suffocating in these tangles. And in the morning it was the emptiness that surprised him. This deserted alleyway in Port-Vendres (just over the border), a few hours after the last shots of the war had been fired, a few miles away from bombed towns and howling crowds, this open ground-floor window, a woman ironing linen, her daughter out in the street holding up a doll and placing it on the windowsill, the soft hiss of the water beneath the iron, the steam with its poignant aroma of a happy life. It would take him several months to get used to these oases of happiness and routine, the snares of forgetfulness.

In Paris he tried to people this void with the glib excitement of the cinema, went to see all the latest films and at one performance noticed a woman in the audience weeping: the screen heroine was sobbing her heart out, her face immaculate as she looked up from a letter. He lost track of the plot, thinking back to the streets of Barcelona, a distraught mother with a dead child in her arms . . . On the way out he was amused to notice a young fair-haired woman through an office window talking on the telephone, her head rendered monstrous by a gas mask. It was funny and also upsetting to him because the young woman strongly resembled his fiancée. He had just received a letter from her breaking off their engagement, reproaching him for his involvement in Spain, for his by now intolerable absence and for what she called, 'your vagabond streak'. He smiled, wryly. Inside the window a man was adjusting the gas mask on the blonde woman's head. She turned her tapir's muzzle towards him. It was funny after all. He promised himself to tell his family about it; he was due to see them at the beginning of September.

\*     \*     \*

The day he reached the family home was the day war was declared. His sixteen-year-old brother could hardly contain his delight: he dreamed of becoming a ship's captain. Jacques Dorme even heard him exclaim: 'Let's hope it lasts for a bit!' He said nothing, knowing that to really fear and hate war you had to have fought in one. At the moment of his departure his mother doubtless uttered almost the same words as she had addressed to her husband in 1914. The portrait of his father was still in the same place in the drawing-room, only now this man, photographed a year before he went off to the front, struck Jacques Dorme as astonishingly young. And indeed he really was younger than his son.

During the course of that sleepless night at Stalingrad in May 1942 he recalled the incident of the fair-haired girl in the gas mask and recounted it to the woman he had just met in amongst the trains. They laughed at the thought of the strange grunting sounds her lover might have found himself listening to at the other end of the line. And, in a moment of vertigo, he had a vision of everything that lay between him and that day in Paris, everything that in less than two years had turned him into another being, all the density of life and death that he had had to ingest. From an August day in Paris, coming out of the cinema, to this great wooden house, half destroyed by bombing, this woman, a stranger yet suddenly so close to him, this township beyond the Volga, the terrible convulsions of a country preparing to fight for its life and the boundless calm of these moments, of that star in the breach in the wall, of the scent exhaled by those white clusters in the darkness.

And this giddiness at the thought of what has brought him all the way to this spot.

He would try to talk of it that night, amid the chaos of his memories, of things forgotten, of admissions that took him by surprise. From time to time, there would be a silence, they would look at one another, bonded by the awareness of the extreme inadequacy of words.

The silences also covered up his reluctance to admit that he had more than once gambled with his life. He spoke of 'blazing streamers' to describe bursts of tracer bullets in the nights of the air battles in May and June 1940. After remarking that the pilots in his squadron had been fighting one against five, he immediately checked himself, afraid to sound boastful, and conjured up the ribbons of fiery streamers in which the German fighter force entangled them. As if at a carnival ball . . .

As for his last engagement, again Jacques Dorme told her about it in few words, mainly to explain that his presence there, at a marshalling yard, in a Russian city, was ultimately due to his bloody-minded determination to catch up with a German bomber, a Heinkel that had unloaded its two tons of death and was simply returning to base, as one goes home after work. On a fine afternoon in June . . . The advantage in speed his Bloch had over the German was minimal; he knew the chase would take time. He had little ammunition left: he would have to approach prudently, avoiding the bomber's many machine guns, manoeuvre faultlessly, fire without counting on a second chance. It took him an interminable time to close in and refine the angle of attack so that by the end it was as if he had known the Heinkel's pilot for an age and could guess the thoughts of this man within the glinting cockpit . . . Even as he shot him down he still had this strange feeling of a personal bond, which generally did not have time to form amid the frenzy of brief duels with fighter planes. Amid his satisfaction at the task accomplished this barely formulated notion crossed his mind: the lives of the pilot and the crew, the final seconds of their lives . . . At this very moment he came under attack, as if by way of a stinging reprimand. No daydreaming! The transparency of the window became iridescent with streaks of oil fanning out, the wind whistled into his pierced shell, the outline of a Messerschmitt slowly appeared in a steep, vertical dive. He managed to climb out onto the fuselage, lost consciousness, came to as a prisoner.

His account of this last battle is interrupted by the dull, rhythmic throb of a heavy train passing in the dark. A train travelling eastwards. Jacques Dorme falls silent and they both pause to listen to the panting sound and, from one coach to the next, a groan of pain, a cry, an abusive response to that cry. The freshness of the air is mingled with the brackish residue of wounds.

'In any case I don't think I'd have had enough fuel for the return flight. I was already operating a long way behind enemy lines, I'd got carried away . . .' She senses that he is smiling in the darkness. As if to excuse himself for having spoken about his victory, the contortion he went through to wrest his plane out of a spin, his fainting. For having talked about it in the proximity of these coaches packed with thousands of soldiers hovering on the brink of death. He smiles.

If love has a beginning, it must, for Alexandra, have been that slight invisible smile in the darkness.

During the months of captivity his thoughts often went back to those days in May and June 1940 and what struck him every time was the vast amount of sky. That was all there had been during those weeks of dogfights, no recollection of what was happening on the ground, no encounters in the town streets, just this blue. Shattered archipelagos of cloud, a blue infinity from which the earth had vanished. His memory was not deceiving him: with several sorties a day, and brief periods of sleep all haunted by these same sorties, it was a simple fact that he rarely had the leisure to find himself on solid ground.

Now, in the confined space of the camp, the earth's clinging gravitational pull dragged at the soles of his feet. And by night the smell of fresh clay stagnated in their hut, pricking his nostrils with its humid acidity. And yet they were privileged, he and the three Polish pilots with whom he shared this low building beside a farm, now transformed into a prisoner-of-war camp. He had spent time in various other places, first of all in Germany, before ending up here, on the eastern frontier of defeated Poland. Everyone sensed that another war was already brewing. These captive pilots could be useful. The German officers who came to inspect them from time to time gave them to understand that henceforth they all had a common enemy and that between civilized people it would always be possible to reach an understanding. So they were entitled to the same food as the guards and to this dwelling where, instead of bunks, each of them had a bed at his disposal. They were free to come and go throughout the camp without special authorization.

In the course of these wanderings Jacques Dorme saw the ordinary prisoners' huts on the far side of the road and one day, for the first time in his life, an execution by hanging – one of the hanged men was very tall: his toes stuck into the earth like the point of a top, his body spun round upon itself several times before growing slack . . . Jacques Dorme experienced a vague feeling of shame, resenting this status of a military aristocracy enjoyed by the pilots.

It was in that camp across the road during the summer of 1941 that he noticed a long column of Russian soldiers and thus learned that the other war, the one everyone had been waiting for, had just broken out.

One night the earth smell that dogged him was unbearable. He got up, crossed the room in the dark, went to open the door and suddenly noticed a glimmer of light behind the pile of old crates, then the silhouette of one of the Poles. That was where the smell came from. Seeing themselves caught in the act, the men made no further attempt at concealment. At the corner of the house a hole opened out into the ground. A head appeared there, eyes blinking in the glow of a match. The Poles looked at one another. Without exchanging any words, as if it was quite simply his turn, Jacques Dorme began helping them to shift the earth from the tunnel.

They escaped on a night of torrential rain at the start of the autumn. The guards did not dare set foot outside, the searchlights looked like the glaucous illuminations of some bathyscaphe, smells and footprints were swallowed up in the mud. One of the pilots, Witold, knew the area well. The next day they reached a village, where they spent two days hidden in a peasant's cellar. He it was who warned them that a search was being organized to recover the fugitives. They had time to escape but on entering the forest had an argument: Witold wanted to press on towards the east, the other two proposed to mark time, wait, prepare for winter. Jacques Dorme went with Witold and that is how after several nights' march they crossed the Russian frontier, without at first being aware of it, and found themselves in the unstable and deceptive world that lies behind a war's front line.

They came upon villages where the orchards were heavy with fruit but the streets were peopled with corpses, like that hamlet in the Kiev region where a dozen women who had been shot looked as if they were resting after a day of harvesting. They skirted the towns during the night, and would sometimes hear German songs, drunken voices. One day they found themselve within a stretch of territory that was surrounded, passed Russian units but did not attempt to make contact with them: this was no longer an army but fragments of human flotsam, clinging to one another, pushing one another aside into the mud, snatching food from one another, falling, shot down by officers struggling to halt the retreat, shooting the officers to clear a path for themselves. Amid this disorderly torrent there were pockets of astonishing stability: detachments, isolated and without hope of assistance, that dug shelters, gathered arms, prepared their defence.

When the running noose was drawn tight and every

direction became equally dangerous to take, they hid among the dead on a battlefield. The German regiments passed by just a few yards away from them, sometimes the mocking laughter of a mouth organ floated over on the breeze, but there were so many bodies strewn across the plain, in the trenches, behind the shattered timbers of a fortified position, that it would have taken a whole army to flush out these two living men: the tall red-haired Pole, stretched out in a shell crater, and the dark-haired French-man, watching the passing lorries through half-closed eyes. At night, to forget about the rustling of the wings ceaselessly flapping above the corpses, they talked at length in their habitual mixture of Polish, Russian, German and French. They were both amazed to see the Germans already thrust-ing so deeply into the heart of Russia. 'If they continue like this,' observed Witold, 'they'll cut off the Volga. And for the Russians the Volga is like . . .' He drew the edge of his hand across his throat, by the carotid artery. They also remarked to one another that for weeks now there had no longer been any Russian planes to be seen in the sky.

At the start of the winter they were captured and then adopted by a group of partisans living in an encampment hidden away amid forest and marshland. Once the period of suspicion had passed, their involvement was accepted and Jacques Dorme now discovered an invisible war, tucked away beneath the humus of the forest, an often clumsy struggle, since it was waged by elderly peasants armed with ancient rifles, but which in the long term wore down the enemy more than conventional attacks would have done. He also noted that in this war an infinitely more violent hatred prevailed than he had experienced in the air.

On one occasion they succeeded in driving the Germans out of a village and found a crowd of naked women and children, standing upright at a crossroads under falling snow: bodies transformed beneath a stream of water into a frozen cluster. This was, no doubt, the response to what could sometimes be seen at roadsides: a German soldier, stripped bare, an ice statue likewise, with an uplifted, frozen arm, pointing in the direction marked on a sign hung about his neck: 'Berlin'. Or had the idea for this come first from the occupying power? Catching the look of a peasant who had recognized his wife in the group turned to ice, Jacques Dorme perceived that this question had by now become meaningless.

In March 1942 an aircraft that came to deliver arms to the partisan camps took the two pilots on board. As the plane became airborne they started singing for joy. Jacques Dorme no longer knew what language he was singing in.

Here was how they had pictured the end of their odyssey: an airfield, a row of fighter planes, mechanics busying them-selves with the aircraft and a squadron commander asking them to show what they could do, before accepting them.

What happens to them is not too far removed from what they had hoped for. There is a stretch of land suggestive of an airfield but it is empty, all that can be seen is the outline of a Russian Pe-2 bomber, without its undercarriage, its fuselage riddled with holes. A few wooden huts serve as hangars, but not a single mechanic is at work there. There is, however, a bustle of soldiers, who seem to be preparing to evacuate the area. And planes can be heard in the sky, above the town. The pilots recognize them: 'Junkers 87.

Yes, dive-bombers . . .' They are then locked up in one of the hangars and try not to interpret this as a bad sign. The door opens: flanked by two soldiers, the person they had hoped would be the squadron commander appears. He is a thin little man, dressed in black leather, with a cross-belt. His greatcoat and boots gleam in the sun. He does not greet them, announces that they will be interrogated separately, points at Witold and says to the guards: 'Bring him . . .'

Jacques Dorme watches what happens through a broad crack between the planks of the wall. In the middle of the courtyard a wooden table and two benches can be seen. The man in black leather sits down, Witold prepares to do the same but the soldiers seize him, force him to stand. The place suddenly begins to look like one of those indeterminate backyards we wander through in our nightmares. There is this table, in bright sunlight, amid the trampled snow. Soldiers carry crates, cans of petrol, cooking pans: they cross the courtyard, paying no attention to the interrogation, and disappear at the other end. The roar of the aircraft sometimes becomes deafening, then stops for a moment and one can hear the noisy trickle of drops sliding off the roof, still heavy with ice. The man in leather shouts an order and the bustle of the men carrying things comes to a halt. All that can be seen now is the interrogation table and an army lorry parked under a tree.

When the aircraft noise fades, Jacques Dorme manages to catch certain words, but senses that, more than the words, it is the difference between these two men that counts and will determine the outcome: the pilot, tall, with an open face and a firm voice; the man in black, very neat despite the springtime mud, staring at the Pole with unconcealed hatred. At one moment their voices are raised.

To overcome the droning of the dive-bombers, Jacques Dorme tells himself. But the tone continues to harden even when silence returns. He sees the man in black leather stand up, his two fists leaning on the table. Witold shouts and waves his hands, the soldiers poke him in the ribs with their submachine-guns. Jacques Dorme hears the Pole yelling Stalin's name in a contemptuous outburst. The man in black stands up again, his mouth twists, hisses: 'You filthy spy . . .' several times, and suddenly he starts to draw his revolver. The seconds become unbelievably long. Witold and the two soldiers watch him doing it, unmoving. To Jacques Dorme it seems as if this fixity of stares lasts for at least a minute. The man grasps the gun, everyone has time to realize what is happening, Witold has time to lick his lips. And the shot is fired, then another.

Jacques Dorme knows it is impossible. A man is not killed like this without a trial. It must be a blank cartridge, to inspire fear. You cannot kill a man in front of this table, in this sunlight . . . Witold falls. The man in black leather puts away his pistol, the soldiers drag the body in through the open door of one of the barrack huts.

When he finds himself out there on the bench Jacques Dorme has the strange sensation of not having left his observation post behind the hangar wall, of continuing to observe the scene, of there being quite simply this other man, himself, who will now talk for several minutes, then die. The one looking through the crack ought to do something: hurl himself at the man in black leather, wrest his pistol from him, shout, alert a commanding officer. The man repeats his question, one of the soldiers thrusts the barrel of his submachine-gun into the back of Jacques Dorme's neck, prompting him to speak. He replies, is amazed at the automatic correctness of what he is saying, realizes he is speaking Russian and that it is the first time this language has been quite as useful as this to him. He also has enough presence of mind to appreciate the strangeness of this first time. To appreciate that his replies will not ward off what awaits him and that this knowledge of Russian is the gravest charge against him, against this 'spy', para-chuted in by the Germans, and trying to pass himself off – a likely story! – as a French pilot. In particular, he believes he has identified the man in black leather, not him but the men of this type, whom he came across in Spain. Men in black leather. The Russian airmen, he recalls, used to break off their conversations when one of these men approached and Jacques Dorme could not for the life of him understand this fear in pilots who confronted death ten times a day. They would stiffen and the only explanation they gave was a combination of letters: GPU or else NKVD . . .

The scream of planes going into a nosedive obliterates all words. They face one another in silence, staring into one another's eyes. Suddenly Jacques Dorme senses that the man in leather is very frightened, that these narrow brown eyes are squinting with fear. An aircraft flies over the hangars, dives down on the infantrymen in the next street who are preparing to pull out. There are shouts, the stampeding of a crowd. Jacques Dorme looks up, notices the notched silhou-ette of another plane and in an automatic, instant targeting, assesses the angle, the distance, the approach speed . . . He has an impulse to warn the man in leather, but the latter is already running, running slowly, caught up in the stiff panels of his greatcoat, his hand gripping the holster of his revolver. He ought to get down, throw himself behind a wall, beneath this bench that Jacques Dorme slides under, but the dive-bomber is already passing overhead, bursting their eardrums with its roar, firing.

There is still the same table in the middle of the court-yard, the same sunlight, the ice melting into long, iridescent drops. And now, close to the lorry's running-board, this body in its black leather, huddled up, the smashed head fallen forwards on its chest. 'The man who wanted to kill me . . .' Jacques Dorme says to himself, without yet grasp-ing the sense of his words – 'The man I wanted to save . . .'

He has no time to realize what is happening to him. A cross-country vehicle pulls up in the courtyard, the officer who escorted them this morning gets out and claps him on the shoulder. 'So that's it. He's checked you over, our spycatcher?' Jacques Dorme indicates the lorry with a jerk of his chin. The officer emits a long whistle, followed by a torrent of oaths. He goes to look at the corpse, stoops, retrieves the pistol and explains with a wink: 'He's killed more Russians than Germans with this. Only don't tell anyone I said so . . .' Jacques Dorme tells him about Witold. The same whistle, a bit less long drawn out, the same oaths: 'Poor bloody Polack! What rotten luck . . . No, we haven't time. The Fritzes will be here before nightfall. Get in quick. We need to see Colonel Krymov.' Jacques Dorme refuses, argues. The officer insists, becomes angry, waves the pistol he has just taken from the dead man. Jacques Dorme smiles: 'Go ahead. Shoot. At least that'll be one who's not Russian.' In the end they load Witold's body into the vehicle and drive off, weaving a path between the bomb craters and the skeletons of burning lorries.

Colonel Krymov is nowhere to be found. At the com-mand post they shrug their shoulders, his aide-de-camp advises them to wait. They decide to inspect all the houses, few in number, where lights are visible. The last one they visit is this *izba* where the windows sparkle with a flickering radiance. Before knocking they go up to the window and look in. The room is lit by the ruddy glow from the fire in the big stove. A hefty, naked man can be seen heaving about on the bed, apparently alone; he lets himself fall, full length, rears up again, falls back once more. Suddenly his hand plunges into the hollow of the bed, extracts from it a heavy female breast and kneads it between his fingers. The bed is very deep, much sunken by the weight of the lovers, and the woman's body is buried in the depths of this nest. The man collapses, emerges. This time his hand fishes out a broad thigh, pink from the fire. It is a bed on castors; at each thrust it moves forwards, then backwards, but not as far. A military greatcoat looks as if it is sitting bolt upright on a chair.

They see Krymov at the command post an hour later. He shows them the road to take next day and advises them to set off very early because, 'We'll be in for a merry time here soon.' The dour melancholy with which he says this surprises Jacques Dorme. Merry . . . He does not understand. 'My Russian doesn't stretch to it,' he says to himself.

The frost that night is very light and there is soft earth in the corner of an orchard. When the grave is filled in Jacques Dorme sinks a cross into it: two planks of wood fastened together with wire. 'At long last,' sighs the officer, 'that was well done,' and fires three shots into the air with his pistol.

The pulsating of a whole new lease of life, after being saved in the nick of time, keeps him from sleeping. This thought is uppermost: he will never be able to explain to anyone that the war was all this too.

More echoes of the war could be heard next day in the tones of his latest escort. (Jacques Dorme was getting the feeling that his successive mentors simply did not know how to get rid of him.) This flying officer informed him with a little dry laugh: 'By the way, Krymov's regiment . . . Mincemeat. Not a single one got away. And the village. Not a single house left standing. They put them through the mincer.' A gesture emphasized his words.

The following day they travelled back through the same village, since then recaptured from the Germans, and came upon a young signaller lying dead on the road, close to a length of wire that had been severed in an explosion. His arms torn to pieces by shrapnel, he had clamped the two ends of the wire together in his teeth . . . What seemed to amaze the flying officer more than anything was the soldier's ingenuity.

War was this nimbleness, too.

As was the hallucinatory reappearance, the next morning, of the man in black leather . . .

They had reached the end of a field covered in snow and recognized the airfield they had spent four days searching for. There, beside a heavy three-engined aircraft, the interrogation scene was being repeated, as if in a wounded man's delirious dream. There was this man clad in a long, black leather coat, a man taller than and substantially different from the first, but acting out the same role. Pistol in hand, he was pacing up and down in the middle of a group of officers, uttering threats coupled with oaths, pointing at the aircraft and from time to time tapping on the fuselage. He did not seem to notice the arrival of Jacques Dorme and his guide, the flying officer.

'I know all about your sabotage!' he was yelling. 'I've caught you red-handed. I know you're trying to undermine the decisions of the Supreme Commander . . .' Intermingled with oaths as they were, these accusations had a bizarre ring in Jacques Dorme's ears, with the Supreme Commander, Stalin, finding himself sandwiched between a 'shit!' and a 'fuck-your-mother!' An officer in a pilot's flying suit spoke up in the tones of a schoolboy seeking to excuse himself: 'But, Comrade Inspector, we can't load twice its capacity . . .' There was a further procession of 'fuck-your-mothers' and 'shits' coupled this time with the Party: 'If the Party decides this aircraft can carry three tons that means it can carry three tons! And anyone who opposes the decisions of the Party is a fascist lackey and will be liquidated!' The barrel of the pistol jabbed into the pilot's cheek: he swallowed his saliva and whispered: 'I'm willing to give it one more try but . . .' The man in leather lowered the pistol: 'But it will be your last. The Party will not tolerate the presence of fascist agents in the ranks of our squadrons.'

The pilot and another officer took their places in the aircraft. Jacques Dorme felt as if he were going in with them, imitating each move they made in the cockpit, studying the instrument panel . . . He had recognized the aircraft as soon as he set eyes on it, despite the state it was in: it was a Junkers 52, the very type he had flown in Spain. The machine gun had been removed and the turret dismantled (perhaps so that it could carry the famous three-ton load decided on by the Party . . .). And the outer surface of the fuselage and the wings had been painted a murky blue.

The runway was long enough but the aircraft began to taxi sluggishly, the jolting of the run pulled it down against the ground. A hundred yards before reaching the line of snowdrifts at the end the aircraft reared, raised its nose, then clung to the runway, began to veer round, swerved off towards the virgin snow. The engine fell silent.

The man in leather drew his pistol and began running towards the plane. Everyone followed him but with hesitant steps, not knowing how to avoid the cowardice of involvement. The pilot had climbed out and was standing close to the plane, his eyes on the running man. His comrade was hiding behind it, pretending to examine a propeller.

His voice raw with rage and the cold, the man in leather barked out: 'Not content with disobeying the orders of the Party, you also attempt to destroy military equipment. For this you will all be court-martialled. You too!' He swung round at a flight sergeant who was standing on the sidelines.

At this moment the flying officer intervened, introduced himself, introduced Jacques Dorme. The man in leather stared at them disdainfully, then cried out in shrill tones: 'So what's he waiting for? Let him get in. Let him prove he's a pilot and not a spy parachuted in during the night!'

Jacques Dorme walked round the aircraft, asked to see the cargo. The pilot sighed, opened the door, and they climbed into the dark cabin of the Junkers. The interior was taken up with big wooden crates, piled high with scrap metal: thick cast-iron slabs, tank tracks . . . This test flight had no doubt been devised to measure the maximum load. They climbed out. A crowd formed round Jacques Dorme. There was a steely silence. Gusts of wind could be heard hissing against the blades of the propeller. 'It can be done,' stated Jacques Dorme, 'but there's one thing I shall need . . .'

The man in leather grimaced mistrustfully. 'What more do you want? An auxiliary engine, perhaps?' Jacques Dorme shook his head: 'No, not an engine. I shall need two bars of soap . . .'

There was such a violent explosion of laughter that a flock of rooks clattered up from the roof of a hangar and wheeled off over the fields, as if borne away by a storm. The flying officer was laughing, bent double, the pilot with his face resting against the fuselage of the Junkers, the flight sergeant with his fists pressed to his eyes, the others spinning round, their legs shaking, as if drunk. A cap rolled in the snow, their eyes wept tears. The man in leather danced about among them, thumping them on the back and shoulders with the butt of his pistol . . . In vain, for their laughter sprang from being too close to death. When the spasms finally calmed down, when the officers had stopped pretending to soap their necks and chests, the laughter took hold of the man in leather. He could not help himself, he forced his voice to seem threatening, froze the muscles on his face, but the eruption burst forth from his clenched lips, twisted his waxen mask, he was squealing. The others looked at him in silence, with preoccupied, almost distressed expressions. It was probably in order to save face that, between two of his squeals, he shouted: 'Get him what he wants!'

The aircraft gathered speed, taxied back to the start of the runway and braked. Jacques Dorme jumped to the ground, went round to join the man in the flying suit who had remained among the crates of the cargo. At the other end of the field the inspector could be seen, running towards them, waving his pistol . . . They lifted up one end of a long crate that loomed large right in the middle. Jacques Dorme slid the two pieces of soap under its wooden base, one at each side. 'If you can manage to push it forward,' he said to the man, who was beginning to understand, 'we're saved . . .' And he explained the precise moment when the centre of gravity needed to be manipulated.

The aircraft began its take-off run, passing a few yards away from the man in leather, lifted clear of the earth, just grazing the rim of ice. And began to lose height.

From the ground they could see that the left wing was tilting down, it was losing speed, grinding to a halt, it seemed to them. 'It's a goner!' murmured the flight sergeant. Suddenly, with an abrupt roll, the plane tilted the other way, the right wing now plunging downwards, but less dangerously and losing less momentum. And once more it limped to the left, then once again to the right . . . Thus it gained height, now swaying less and looking more and more like an ordinary aircraft. 'Tossing the pancake!' exclaimed one of the pilots in the group on the runway. And several voices took up the cry, admiringly: 'Tossing the pancake!' The manoeuvre was known to them, as a way of getting overloaded aircraft off the ground, but only real aces could bring it off.

In the belly of the Junkers sat the man in the flying suit, leaning his back against a long crate arranged at an angle. His eyes were reddened, he was panting jerkily. When he recovered his breath he got up and crawled towards a window. Down below lay the winding course of a river, grey beneath the ice, the airfield was no longer visible. He opened the door and began throwing out pieces of scrap metal, then, shoving it along the soapy floor, a whole crate. 'That way we've a better chance of landing, with that madman . . .' He pricked up his ears. The pilot was singing. In a language unknown to him.

At the end of April Jacques Dorme learned that he was going to be posted to a completely new squadron, a special unit that would fly American planes from Alaska across Siberia. He was disappointed. He had hoped to be taken on as a fighter pilot, to go and fight at the front. One detail consoled him: flying this route, over three thousand miles long, was considered to be much more dangerous than operating over enemy lines.

During those weeks of waiting he often found himself thinking again about the impossibility of explaining the war: telling himself that after the event everyone would talk about it, publish commentaries, accusations, justifications. Everyone, and above all, those who had not fought in it. Everything would be crystal clear at last: enemies, allies, the righteous and the monsters. The years of fighting would be recorded, day after day, in terms of troop movements, glorious battles. The essential truth would be forgotten: that the whole of wartime was made up of myriad moments of war and that sometimes behind the vast turmoil of the fronts there lurked a sunlit courtyard, a March day, where a man in black leather killed another man because he felt like killing. And that on the very same day there would be a certain Colonel Krymov, a naked man, quickly satisfying his lust for the flesh of a woman before being cut to pieces by machine gun fire. And also that young man, his jaws clenched around the telegraphic cable . . . He soon lost his way among his recollections and this led him to conclude that the vital thing was to keep all these fragments of war in one's memory, all these tiny wars fought by soldiers long forgotten.

At the beginning of May he crossed the Volga at Stalingrad and recalled Witold's words: 'For the Russians, the Volga is like . . .' He got off the train too soon by mistake and spent a long time walking along the tracks at a marshalling yard. Through the smoke from a tank wagon set on fire by incendiary bombs he saw a woman directing the chaotic traffic. 'Here is yet another war,' he thought. 'This woman, so beautiful, so poorly clad, so soon forgotten . . .' He did not immediately grasp that he was the one the woman was shouting at.

# Six

I was thirteen that summer when Alexandra talked to me about the French pilot. The questions I asked were about the maximum speed of the Bloch aircraft, the operating range of the bomber Jacques Dorme had shot down, the type of pistol the man in the black leather greatcoat was armed with, the gas mask that allowed you to talk on the telephone (the ones we used during paramilitary exercises at the orphanage offered no such possibility) . . . She smiled, confessing her ignorance of such matters.

Years later I would come to know what her smile had left unspoken: the infinite distance between what aroused my curiosity and her life of only a few days with Jacques Dorme. She could not tell me about their love. Because of my age, I would at first think, lamenting the stupidity of that age, focused as it is on the minutiae of warfare and bold strategic initiatives. Because of her old-fashioned modesty, I would later tell myself, regretting the elusiveness of those few furtive moments in May 1942 which her story had scarcely allowed me to glimpse. And then one day I would come to realize that nothing more could have been said about that love. And that those moments ('she talked to me about what the weather was like', I thought bitterly more than once), those random recollections of rain or of a misty morning, were enough and told the essential truth about this brief and simple love affair. As the years passed, I learned to read them better, to conjure up their light, to hear the wind and the hiss of the rain coming in through the breach in the wall, transmitting its chill right over to the bed. This love, never referred to, came to reveal itself and ripen in me as I grew older. As did the moment when the old amber bead necklace snapped, which had at first been merely evocative to me of a night of rain and wind.

The wind banishes the sultry, resinous heat of the steppes, the smell of burning oil, the dense breath of human beings crammed into hundreds of railway carriages. As the rain-drops begin to patter down on the floor through the breach they suddenly blend in with the clatter of the beads from the broken necklace. For a moment the bodies pause in their amorous struggle, their breathing stilled, then all at once they fuse again, lost in a tempo quickened by desire, letting the beads beat time as they slip from the thread.

I needed to have lived to understand both the rain and the blissful weariness that permeated the woman's move-ments as she rose, went over to the breach, lingered in the warm, fluid embrace of the storm. To understand the measured pace of the remarks that were obliterated by the downpour's noisy torrent, to perceive that what was important was precisely this measured pace and not the sense of the words spoken. To understand that these lost remarks, the bliss of these slow movements, the scent of the wild cherry, mingled with the acidity of the lightning flashes, all these elements, not retained in any memory, amounted to the essence of a life, one that the two lovers had truly lived, which was the first thing doomed to disappear into oblivion.

\*     \*     \*

Also hidden behind those recollections of 'what the weather was like' there was that other night, the hypnotic stillness of the air, the static density of a storm that does not break. They go down, cross the tracks, walk out from the township that lies unmoving in the darkness, like scenery in a closed theatre, set out along a sandy path across the steppe. The silence allows them to hear the rustle of every footfall and, when they stop, the faint crackling of bone-dry plants. The heat casts a veil over the stars; they seem more alive, less severe towards human brevity. At one moment an anti-tank obstacle raises its crossed steel girders. They finger these iron bars rearing up in the darkness. The metal is still hot from the day's sunlight. In the torpor of the night these metal crosses, strung out in a line, look like the relics of some ancient, forgotten war. They say nothing, knowing the thought is unavoidable: a line of defence on the far side of the Volga, a willingness to envisage the war crossing the Volga, engulfing its left bank, strangling Stalingrad. They think this and yet the soldered steel seems to derive from a past history with no relevance to this night. They walk on in silence, with a physical sense that the ties binding them to the houses of the township, to the labyrinth of tracks in the marshalling yard, to their lives back there, are growing weaker. There is only the chalky gleam of the path, the darkness tinged with blue by the silent flickering of lightning flashes and suddenly, there at their feet, the abyss of this night sky, the stars floating on the black surface of the water.

It is one of the seasonal oxbow lakes that appear in the spring with the melting of the snows, only to be swallowed in a few gulps by the steppe during the summer drought. Its fleeting existence is for the moment at its most abundant. The water fills its ephemeral banks to the brim, the clay smell seems as if it has always hung there. And the body, as it dives in, is tickled by the long stems of yellow water lilies, firmly rooted.

They remain for a whole hour in this sluggish flow, scarcely moving, starting to swim, then lingering at the centre of the water's shallow expanse. The silent flashes of lightning last long enough for them to see one another, for him to see this woman with wet hair, her hands smoothing a face upturned towards the stars. To see the woman's closed eyes. To see her stretched out on the shore, where the fine, smooth soil seems to be heated deep below the surface.

'If it had not been for this war I should never have met you . . .' The man's voice is at once very close, like a whisper in the ear, and lost in the remoteness of the steppes. It must be audible even there, on the horizon where the summer lightning glimmers. 'No, that's not what I meant to say,' he corrects himself. 'You see, this plain, this water, this night. All this is so simple and, in fact, this is all we need. This is all anyone needs. And yet the war will come all the way here . . .' He falls silent, feels the woman placing her hand on his arm. A bird flies by, they can hear the hushed stirring of the air. It feels to them as if this war now so imminent has already passed over these steppes, bringing destruction and death, and has finally evaporated into the void. They will be living through it soon, to be sure, and yet one part of them is already beyond it, already in a night where the recently-erected steel obstacles are nothing more than rusting relics. Where there is nothing left but the soundless glittering of the horizon, this star in a footprint filled with water, the face of the woman, leaning over him, the caress of the damp ends of her hair. A post-war night, endless.

*   *   *

In their life of just over a week together there was also that morning blinded by fog. Not a plane in the sky, no risk of air-raids, trains advancing at a sleepwalker's slow pace. The women who worked with Alexandra had let her go, had almost forced her to take this morning off, for they had learned, or guessed, that it was her last.

It was cold, more like an autumn morning. A cool, misty day in May. They walked along beside a meadow, passed through a village from which the inhabitants had just been evacuated. The presence of the river was given away in the fog by the dull echo of the void and the scent of rushes. One of the mornings in their life . . . They sensed that it was the moment to speak grave, definitive words, words of farewell and hope, but what came to mind seemed heavy and pointless. What needed to be admitted was that this single week had been a long life of love. During it time had vanished. The pain to come, absence, death, would leave this life unblemished. This needed to be said. Yet they held their peace, certain it was a sentiment they shared, down to the tiniest nuance.

Invisible, in the cotton-wool blindness of the fog, a boat passed, close to the bank, they could hear the oars slipping lazily into the water, the rhythmic groan of the rowlocks.

During the hours they lived through together Alexandra had told Jacques Dorme the story I was to hear as a child. A young Frenchwoman's arrival in Russia in 1921 as a member of a Red Cross mission, a temporary visit, or so she had thought, which became more and more irreversible as the country very rapidly cut itself off from the world.

What they talked about, in fact, was four different countries: two Russias and two Frances. For the Russia

Jacques Dorme had just travelled through, a Russia broken by defeat, was hardly known to Alexandra. As for her France, that of the days following the Great War and the start of the twenties, her memories had long since blended with the sweet and often illusory shade of the homeland she dreamed of. He had known a quite different country.

One day, thanks to a news bulletin they happened to hear on the radio, these two Frances came into collision.

They had lunch together that day. When there was a break in the flow of trains beneath the windows and the hum of the aircraft died away, they could imagine they were lunching in peacetime on a sunny spring day . . . They were just about to part when, with a mysterious air, Alexandra murmured: 'This evening I shall need your help. No, no, it's very serious. You must put on a white shirt, polish your shoes and have a good shave. It's a surprise . . .' He smiled, promising to come dressed to the nines. It was then that they heard the radio announcer's voice, reporting in grim, metallic tones that the town of Kerch had fallen and speaking of fierce fighting in the defence of Sebastopol . . . They knew this news implied the impending loss of the Crimea and a German breakthrough to the south, which would open a route to the Volga. The radio also reported that the Allies were in no hurry to open a 'second front'. Perhaps these were the words that set the match to the powder keg.

Alexandra spoke in harsh, mocking tones that were new to him. She affected amazement at the casual attitude of the Americans and the caution of the English, sitting tight on their battleship island. And, still more bitterly, she declared herself sickened by France, by the spinelessness of her military leaders, by the treachery of her government. No doubt she carried in her mind a memory of the army, bled white but triumphant, at the victory parade of 1919. As for that of 1940 . . . She spoke of cowardice, evasion, an easy life paid for by shifty compromises. 'But we fought . . .' Jacques Dorme did not raise his voice as he said it. He spoke in the tones of one who accepts the other's arguments, merely seeking to bear witness to the facts.

How a serving Frenchman like him might have replied to her I shall never know. Did he describe the battle of the Ardennes? The fight for Flanders? Or perhaps the air battles in which his own comrades in the squadron had perished? At all events he appeared to be justifying himself. Alexandra cut him short. 'At least let me picture a country that rises up as a whole and drives out the Boche, instead of making pacts with them. Yes, a country that fights back. What the Russians are doing. It's already clear that the Germans are not unbeatable. But of course if people don't want to put themselves in danger . . .'

'You're saying what they'll say after the war. What people will say who didn't fight in it.' Jacques Dorme's voice remained calm, a little drier perhaps. Infuriated, Alexandra almost shouted: 'And they'll be right to say it! For if the French had really decided to fight . . .'

'If they had really decided to do so, here's what you'd have had where France is now . . .'

Jacques Dorme took the map of the world from a shelf, spread it out on the table among the plates from lunch and repeated: 'Here's what you'd have had . . .' He held a box of matches in his hand and this covered the purple hexagon of France almost completely, with only the western tip of Brittany and the Alpine fringe showing. Then the matchbox flew over Europe and landed on the USSR, on the territory conquered by the Nazis. There was room on this for four matchboxes. 'Four times the size of France . . .' he said in grim tones. 'And I'll tell you something. I've seen every one of these four Frances devastated, towns razed to the ground, roads covered in corpses. I've travelled across them, these four lands of France. That's just to tell you what the Boche army can do. As for the Russians, I've seen all kinds. I've even seen one whose arms had been cut to ribbons by shrapnel and who had his teeth clamped round a broken telephone line, copper against copper, wrapped in a scrap of cloth, in accordance with instructions. And he died with his teeth clenched . . . They're going to lose ten million men in this war, maybe even more. Lose them, do you understand? Ten million . . . That's the total number of able-bodied men France had to give.'

He folded up the map, put it back on the shelf. And in a voice once more calm, no longer judgemental, he added: 'And, by the way, we didn't have a "second front" in May 1940 either . . .'

That evening he arrived dressed in a white shirt, his cheeks smooth, his shoes well polished. They smiled at one another, and when they spoke avoided any return to the subject of their quarrel. 'It's a little surprise. You'll see,' she told him again as they set out. The previous day the director of the military hospital had asked her to take part in a concert that was being organized prior to the evacuation of all the wounded, now that the front was drawing nearer. Several women would be singing, he explained, and then a couple would dance a waltz – he was counting on her for this. The concert hall had been set up, not in the hospital, which was too cluttered with beds, but in an engine shed, from which the locomotives had been withdrawn for the evening.

As they made their way inside, she recoiled in shock. The surprise was greater for her than for him. Hundreds of pairs of eyes were focused on the still-empty platform, countless tightly-packed rows of men sitting there, at once all different and all resembling one another. The living mass of them extended right to the back of this long brick building and was lost in the darkness, giving the impression of stretching away, row upon row, to infinity. She was accustomed to seeing them divided up into separate wards, overcrowded, of course, but where the multiplicity of their injuries and suffering was matched by individual faces. Here, in this vast parade of pain, all the eye could see was an undifferentiated mass of tissue in torment. Studded with pale heads, white with bandages.

Half a dozen women sang in chorus, unaccompanied. Their voices sounded naked; even in the cheerful songs they tugged at the heartstrings, too close to tears. The applause was muted: many arms in slings, stumps where arms should be.

Now it was their turn. A nurse placed a chair at the side of the stage. Two soldiers came on and set down a legless amputee, a young man with bright red hair and a dashing air. They brought him an accordion. As if in a dream, Alexandra and Jacques Dorme stepped up onto the boards which smelled of fresh timber.

Their bodies' memories quickly overcame the fear of not recalling the steps. The accordion player played with an imperceptibly delayed waltz tempo, as if he would have liked to see them dancing for as long as possible. As they revolved, they saw the blaze of his hair and this devastating contrast: a broad smile, gleaming teeth and eyes brimming with distress. Briefly and intermittently they also noticed the looks of the wounded men, lines of sparks burning into their bodies as they danced. No trace remained of their lunchtime argument. All talk was charred to a cinder by these looks. An aircraft passed very low overhead, drowning the music for several seconds. They continued spinning amid this hubbub, then, as one dives into a wave, fell back into the melody as it returned.

They felt in the end as if they were alone, dancing in an empty hall, each one's face reflected in the other's eyes. Several times she lowered her eyelids to banish her tears.

Two days later there came that cold, misty morning and, in the evening, his departure. Before boarding the train he had already mingled with the members of what would be his squadron now, his new life. The train moved off, the men talked louder, more cheerfully, it seemed. She just had time to catch sight of his face once more, alongside the grinning countenance of a big fellow who was waving to someone on the platform, then the night blended the carriages into a single dark wall . . . On the way home she listened within herself to the words he had spoken that morning as they walked beside the river. 'After the war, you know, you must think about coming back to the old country . . . Of course they'll let you leave. You'll be a Frenchman's wife. That's if you'll agree to marry me, naturally. That means you'll become a Frenchwoman again and I'll show you my home town and the house where I was born . . .'

She spoke slowly, breaking off to listen to the wind as it scoured the steppe or to let her gaze follow a bird across the July sky. Or did these pauses, perhaps, correspond in her memory to the long months that brought no news of Jacques Dorme? I allowed my eyes to travel along the narrow stream that cast a cooling veil about us, beyond the foliage of the willows and alders that sheltered us beneath their restless network. The banks were cracked in the heat, the almost unmoving brook seemed to be dwindling before our very eyes, sucked dry by the sun. In its place I pictured a broad stretch of water one May long ago, a nocturnal lake and the figures of the two swimmers silhouetted against the blue light of a silent thunderstorm.

There were few things left for her to tell me. She did not talk about the fighting at Stalingrad, knowing that they told us tales of it every year at school, backed up by eyewitness accounts from old soldiers. Nor about the hell behind the lines, in townships transformed into vast field hospitals. After Jacques Dorme's departure and in the course of the three years of his flights across Siberia she had received four letters. Passed from hand to hand, thanks to servicemen on the move: the only means of sending mail from the arctic wastes where his squadron was based and, especially, of thwarting the vigilance of the spycatchers.

The work of the pilots on the 'Alaska-Siberia' line, the 'Alsib', was doubly secret. During the war it had to be concealed from the Germans. After the war from the Soviet people themselves: the cold war had just begun and it was vital for the people not to know that the American imperialists had supplied their Russian ally with over eight thousand aircraft for the Eastern Front. All Alexandra ever learned came from those four letters, a single photo and conversations with a comrade Jacques Dorme had asked to look her up, a task the men of the squadron used to undertake on one another's behalf, with their nearest and dearest in mind. There was also the journey she was to attempt at the beginning of the fifties, in the hope of finding the place where he had died. She brought little back from this: the memory of a barely accessible region, criss-crossed here and there by the barbed-wire fences of the camps and, in response to her questions, prudent silence, ignorance either real or feigned.

Yet she succeeded in making me picture – almost relive – the era of this air bridge hidden from the world. Among the routes I have travelled or dreamed of in my life, that of the Alsib was one of the first to imprint its vertiginous space within me. Three thousand miles from Alaska to Krasnoyarsk in the heart of Siberia, a score of airfields located on the permafrost of the tundra and their names as mysterious as those of staging posts on a quest: Fairbanks, Nome, Uelkal, Omolon, Seymchan . . . The violence of the arctic winds that knocked men over, dragging them across ice where the hand could find nothing to hold onto. The air, at minus sixty, a mouthful of which was like biting into a volley of razor-blades.

Squadrons that relieved one another from one airfield to the next, without days of rest, with no right to weakness, never using the excuse of bad weather, magnetic storms, or the overloading of aircraft. The landing runways built by the prisoners from the camps, the surrounding areas studded with their frozen corpses that nobody bothered to count. The only count kept related to the number of aircraft flown by each of the pilots: more than three hundred by Jacques Dorme, according to his letter dated September 1944. And, a more discreet addendum, the tally of pilots killed in crashes: over a hundred deaths, to which, on New Year's Day 1945, was added his own.

Alexandra had probably guessed a good deal more than the letters and conversations revealed. Moreover, she had not joined in the New Year's Eve celebration with railway colleagues on 31 December 1944. A patient, sly prescience was choking her. It was as if a voice had fallen silent over there within the icy confines of Siberia, a voice that was no longer responding. When, some months later, a friend of Jacques Dorme came to her house and told her the truth, she did not dare mention that presentiment, afraid he might see it as mere 'old wives' superstition'. When she came to tell me about it, it was with a sad little smile, and I would blush, not daring to tell her how much I believed her, believed every word she said, especially about that foreboding, which proved to me how deeply they had loved one another.

In those days I did not have a better definition of love (and I do not know if I have now) than that of a kind of silent prayer which continuously bonds two human beings, separated by space or by death, into an intuitive sharing of the sorrows and moments of joy each experiences.

Sorrow for him, one day, came from examining a heavy Douglas C-47 they had managed to track down as one does a wounded animal, following a trail of blood: despite a snowstorm on the rocky slope the plane had smashed into, there was this long, tawny streak, the colour of fuel, standing out in the middle of the endless white. A warm colour in this world of ice. Warm lives, suddenly destroyed, whose faces and voices Jacques Dorme still remembered . . . Shaking hands with the pilot who, before he climbed into the aircraft, had been telling him about his three-year-old son back in Moscow. A warm handshake.

In cold like this all liquids froze within the bowels of the aircraft. Oil solidified into jelly. And even steel became fragile as glass. The air strove to dissolve the planes into its own crystalline substance. The pilots travelled very close to the zone that broke all records for cold on earth. 'Minus seventy-two degrees,' Jacques Dorme had announced to his Russian mechanic, with a touch of pride.

Joy was discovering a technique for combating the encrustation of ice that grew thicker in flight and little by little coated the entire aircraft. You had to alter the engine speed regularly: as it varied, the vibrations shattered the crust of ice.

Joy was the idea that another ten planes were on their way to Stalingrad, where the outcome of the battle might depend on the arrival of these ten aircraft in the nick of time. Or even that of the single fighter plane he himself was flying, this Aircobra, weighed down, thanks to Siberian distances, by a six-hundred-litre ferry tank beneath the fuselage. He was no fool, he knew that in the monstrous hand-to-hand struggle between two armies, between the millions of men killing one another at Stalingrad, this scrap of sheet metal with a propeller could hardly tip the scales. And yet on each flight an irrational conviction returned: this is the plane that will prevent the destruction of an old wooden house with wild cherry boughs beneath its windows.

In April 1944 he became what, in the pilots' language, they called a 'leader'. Now at the controls of a bomber – a Boston or a Boeing 25 – he was guiding ten or fifteen Aircobras, with a quite different sense of the weight of this little squadron in the scales of the war.

Joy resided in the confidence others had in him, by the resurgent light of the polar sun, that was now showing itself for longer and longer periods. In the devotion of the people on the ground, who would mark out the runways with fir branches when there were blizzards. And also in the thought that these missions at the end of the world were bringing the liberation of his native land closer.

One day he had occasion to suffer a shock such as no brush with death would have administered. He had just landed and, still numb from several hours of flying, saw a column of prisoners walking along beside the airfield. During the course of a week these men had been breaking the ice from dawn until dusk, installing steel plates and covering them with gravel for new runways. That evening they were moving off in single file amid the snowdrifts. The guards surrounded them, training their submachine-guns on this mass of human beings, chilled to the bone and staggering with weariness. Jacques Dorme watched their progress and tried to catch the other pilots' eyes, but the latter turned away, in a hurry to settle down out of the wind, to eat . . . A submachine-gun spat just at the moment when he, too, was about to step inside. He had seen what happened prior to this gunshot. A prisoner had slipped and, to avoid falling, had moved out a little from the line of walking men. With no hesitation a guard fired, the guilty man fell, the column froze for a second, then continued its jolting progress. Jacques Dorme rushed up to the guard, shook him, gave vent to his anger with a shout. And heard a level voice: 'Just following the rule.' Then, more quietly, in tones of hate-filled contempt: 'Want a couple in the balls, too, do you?' One of the pilots took Jacques Dorme by the arm and led him firmly towards the rest of the squadron personnel.

During the meal he sensed a strain in their voices, due both to the impossibility of admitting what had happened, and to shame. Shame that a foreigner had seen it. The only true fact he would learn over supper that evening would be the 'rule' – the words recited automatically by the guards before the column of prisoners sets off: 'One step to the left, one step to the right and I shoot without warning.'

That night, inside the dark cabin of a Douglas transport plane that was taking them back to their base, he stayed awake, his thoughts constantly returning to this strange country whose language he already spoke well, which he thought he knew so well and which he failed to understand – which he sometimes refused to understand. Comparing it to France, he had a thought that left him even more perplexed. This was an occupied country, too. Like France. No, worse than France, for it was occupied from within by the regime that governed it, by the spirit of the rule: 'One step to the left, one step to the right . . .'

The memory of that death stood in the way of the easy joy he had experienced before: in the soft bluish luminescence of the Boston's instrument panels, so much more agreeable than the harsh lighting in Russian aircraft, the almost excessive comfort of the cockpit and, on landing, a system that responded perfectly. Now, when he climbed out onto the runway, the memory of the prisoners in their single file and the man who had stumbled on an icy path came back to him.

At the end of August 1944 he was reminded of that man, but in a new way. That day he was fêted from the morning onwards by all his comrades, pilots and mechanics: they had just learned of the liberation of Paris. As he responded to their congratulations, Jacques Dorme wondered what they knew about France. Amid their excited cries, the Paris Commune and Maurice Thorez kept cropping up, along with the name of Marshal Pétain – uttered with contempt and distorted by the lack of nasal sounds in Russian. He did not even try to explain, feeling himself to be relieved at last of the burden of the fall of France, for which, in conversation, they had sometimes seemed to reproach him. Now they were laughing, remarking that once Hitler had been driven out, the French people would settle the capitalists' hash and set about building communism. A little dazed by their voices, he tried to imagine what kind of books they might have read about France. He recalled Alexandra's tale: the volume she had unearthed in the public library in a Siberian town, the domicile assigned to her. A collection of texts by French authors, translated into Russian, among them a poem that was a veritable 'hymn to the GPU . . .'

During his monotonous flights he pictured Paris, the popular jubilation, windows open to a fine summer sky. And, more than anything, the café terraces, a life spent at tables, garrulous, carefree, made up of snatches of words, exchanged glances, the complicity of bodies brushing against one another . . . Through a thin layer of cloud, beneath the Boston's wings, the mountain peaks came thrusting up from the endless Kolyma plateau, still tinged with green and gleaming with watercourses. 'In a few days' time,' he thought, 'all this will be white. Devoid of life . . .' All that remained would be the rows of rectangles, the barrack huts and watchtowers of a camp, reliable beacons for the pilots in the midst of this mountainous vastness devoid of landmarks. The only point of reference would be these thousands of human lives concentrated together here in this nothingness. In his mind's eye he again pictured the little round tables on the café terraces and reflected that the author of the 'hymn to the GPU' might well be sitting at one of those tables at that very moment, talking to a woman, ordering coffee or wine, commenting on the past, criticizing the present, celebrating the future. Jacques Dorme suddenly realized that you could never make that poet understand the infinity that now lay beneath the wings of the plane, nor the rule: 'One step to the left, one step to the right', nor the death of the prisoner who stumbled . . . No, impossible. He felt something like a muscular spasm locking his jaws. Down there, at their café table, what they were speaking was a different language.

In the course of that flight Jacques Dorme saw himself for the first time as a foreigner in the land of his birth.

He did not immediately recognize the man in black leather. Indeed, this one bore scant resemblance to the little inquisitor who had killed Witold. Still less to the second one, the fat, hysterical one with his orders for an overloaded plane to take off. When the war seemed lost, those two had spread terror; they were more afraid than the servicemen they threatened. The man Jacques Dorme saw in December 1944 already had a victor's self-confidence. He was short and thin, like the first one, but his leather coat was lined with thick fur. He shook its lapels when a little hoar-frost fell on it from a propeller, whose specifications – no one could understand why – were the subject of his enquiries. His curiosity was disconcerting. The pilots felt as if they were undergoing an interrogation in which the excessively simple questions were merely a way of confusing the person interrogated. Occasionally he smiled and Jacques Dorme noticed that at once the smile would vanish from other people's faces.

The man inspected the aircraft, asked his strange questions that would have been considered stupid if they had not contained hidden catches, never listened to the complete answer, smiled. Everyone realized he had come because the war was about to end and back in Moscow they needed to issue a reminder of who was master. However, what the pilots could not yet guess was that soon the Americans, who were supplying these countless Douglases, Boeings and Aircobras, were going to become enemies again and that all those who had taken part in this air bridge would come under suspicion. The man in black leather was already there to spot the straying sheep, to guard against ideological contagion.

At the end of his inspection he summoned those in charge of the base and the 'leaders' of the squadrons. He talked about the slackening of Communist discipline, the lowering of class vigilance, and in particular castigated them over the organization of flights. 'The command staff have tolerated total anarchy,' he rapped out. 'Bombers have been flying in the same groups as fighter aircraft and transport planes. I advise you to put an end to this chaos. Fighter planes must fly with fighters and bombers with . . .'

The pilots exchanged furtive glances, scratching their heads. They were secretly hoping that the man in leather would suddenly burst out laughing and exclaim in jocular tones: 'I had you fooled for a moment!' But his voice remained accusatory and steely. When he spoke of flight plans being incorrectly drawn up, one of the pilots spoke up, belatedly, as if it had taken him time to bring himself to do so: 'But, Comrade Inspector, a Boston has means of communication that are much more . . .' What he intended to say was that a bomber was better equipped with navigational aids than a fighter. The man in black leather lowered his voice, almost to a whisper, and it was this menacing hiss that stopped the pilot short, better than a shout would have done: 'I see, Comrade Flying Officer, that your contacts with the capitalist world have not been wasted on you . . .'

For several moments of heavy silence all that could be heard was the lashing of the blizzard unleashing its fury against the windows, and the crunch of the gravel the prisoners were spreading over one of the runways. Quite physically, in his bones, Jacques Dorme sensed how fine the line was in this country that separated a free man, this flying officer staring in silence at his big hands as they lay on the table, from those prisoners whose only identity was a number stitched onto their padded jackets.

'Well, as for these contacts of yours, we'll see about that after the victory,' the inspector resumed. 'What's needed now is to bring some order into this shambles. Here is the map showing you the most direct routes between airfields. From now on you will travel via Zyryanka and not via Seymchan. This will cut out hundreds of kilometres, with a consequent saving on fuel. I wonder why the squadron commanders haven't thought of it before. But perhaps the longer route was recommended to them by American government representatives . . .'

This time no one said anything. On the map, a straight line, drawn with scholarly application, traced a route that started in Alaska and crossed Siberia. In its geometric logic it passed closer to Zyryanka, one of the auxiliary airfields, far to the north of the normal route. This was more of an emergency runway, envisaged for days when those at Seymchan disappeared beneath snowstorms. The man's pencil had drawn a line right across the terrible Chersky mountain ranges, arctic wastelands, even less explored than the areas currently overflown by the Alsib route . . . Left alone, the pilots stared long and hard at the map with its stubborn pencil line.

The absurdity of it was too evident to be worth mentioning. 'The Party line . . .' murmured the flying officer who had spoken earlier.

They knew the inspector could not return to Moscow without reporting on the subversive activities he had unmasked, the errors he had corrected. That was how the whole country functioned, by denouncing, criticizing, breaking records and exceeding plans. And even at the People's Commissariat of State Security, to which the inspector belonged ('the GPU . . .' thought Jacques Dorme), plans had to be exceeded, you had to arrest more people than in the previous month, shoot more than your colleagues . . .

They talked briefly about the make-up of the flights for the next day then went to get some sleep. Outside in the darkness of the polar night the prisoners went on digging the frozen earth for the new runway.

After an hour in the air Jacques Dorme transmitted this message to the group of aircraft he was leading: 'Take second route. Landing at Z impossible. Divert S.' During the previous night he had managed to persuade the men in his squadron that the best solution was to go, as usual, to Seymchan. He alone would go to Zyryanka, from where he would call the base. The inspector, who was due to leave the following day, would not have time to hold an inquiry.

He veered slowly off to the right and in the ashen gloaming that passed for daylight, saw the lights of the Aircobras turning towards the south.

As the minutes slipped by the man gradually became at one with his aircraft, the shuddering of the steel matched the rhythm of his blood. The pilot's body yielded to the life of the machine, disappeared into the rhythm of the engine at his back, as the throbbing of its vibrations periodically varied. His gaze was lost in the grey light of this day on which the sun would not rise, then returned to the luminous specks on the instrument panel. The man was at once profoundly involved in the motion of this flying cockpit and utterly absent. Or rather present elsewhere, far from this ashen sky and these Chersky mountains that were beginning to pile up tier upon tier of their icy wastes. An elsewhere made up of a woman's voice, a woman's silences, the stillness of a house, of a time he felt he had always inhabited. This time unfolded quite separately from what was happening in the aircraft, around the aircraft. The violence of the wind made it necessary to manoeuvre, the icing-over reduced visibility. At a given moment it became clear that the runways of Zyryanka lay still farther to the north east and that, at the risk of colliding with one of the mountain peaks, he was going to have to fly at a lower altitude, watch, concentrate, not give way to panic. The remoteness he sensed within himself gave him the strength to remain calm, to avoid going into a spin, that curse of the Aircobras, to stop checking the fuel at every moment. Not to sink to the level of being a man anxious to save his own skin at all costs.

He was to hold on to the sensation of that elsewhere right up to the end, right up to the purple luminescence of the northern fire that set the sky ablaze.

Alexandra finished her story as we were making our way home. Dusk was already falling over the steppe. She spoke about the journey she had made to the former Alsib airfields, most of them abandoned after the war, and the peak at the southern end of the Chersky range, three crags clustered together which the local inhabitants called 'the Trident', and which she had failed to reach.

I walked beside her upon the dry grass, an endless rippling expanse that dazzled the eye as, stirred by the wind, it alternated between mauve and gold. The details of her journey stuck in my mind (and this would help me, a quarter of a century later, to locate the places she had told me about) but the astonishment I experienced was caused by something else. A man who had been quite unknown to me a week ago stood before me now, fully realized. Jacques Dorme, whose life story I perceived as a living and luminous whole.

Everyone's perception of mankind and the world has its share of the truth. That of a thirteen-year-old boy walking on the steppe beside the Volga was no less true than my judgement as an adult. It even had a definite advantage: being innocent of psychoanalysis, probings into the mind or sentimental rhetoric, it operated by entities, blocks.

Such was the Jacques Dorme who had appeared to me

in the blaze of that sunset. A man hewn from the very stuff of his native land, that France I had discovered thanks to my reading and my conversations with Alexandra. He was a combination of those qualities that reminded me of 'the finest and purest soldier in old France', the warrior in 'The Last Square', the exiled emperor returning to his native soil on board the ghost ship, and the 'four gentlemen of Aquitaine'. The grain of this human substance was yet more subtle; what I perceived was not the characters and their actions but rather the dense aura of their lives. The spirit of their earthly undertakings. Their soul.

No proofs existed of the accuracy of such a vision. My certainty was enough for me. That, and the photo Alexandra showed me when we reached home. A rectangle with yellowed edges but still retaining the crisp clarity of black and white. A score of pilots, clad in jackets lined with sheepskin and heavy reindeer-skin boots. American airmen recognizable by their lighter clothing, more elegant, more 'pilot as film star'. The photo had probably been taken after a ceremonial parade, for in the corner of the photo the metallic glint of a military band could be seen. No doubt the Soviet and American national anthems had just been played . . . Guided by Alexandra, I located Jacques Dorme. He stood out from the others neither by his physique nor by his clothes (the same three-quarter-length jacket, the same boots). But I could have recognized him without Alexandra's help. Among the pilots who were beginning to break ranks, after standing to attention as required by the anthems, he alone had remained still, his face marked by a certain seriousness, his gaze directed far away. It was as if he could hear a music inaudible to the others, an anthem the band had forgotten to play.

It took me some time to grasp that Jacques Dorme's isolation, despite being surrounded by a crowd, gave him a kinship with the old giant I had seen in front of a monument to the dead, the French general who had broken off in the middle of his speech and allowed his gaze to stray into the immensity of the steppe.

The following evening I left Alexandra's house. I had to return to the orphange, now half-emptied of its past, to prepare myself for a new life. After boarding a crowded suburban train, I managed to catch a glimpse of Alexandra on the platform teeming with holiday-makers. She did not see me, her eyes flitting anxiously along the row of windows. With a hesitant hand she was waving farewell to someone she could not locate among all these faces. To me she looked younger and at the same time somehow defenceless. I thought of another departure, of the train carrying Jacques Dorme towards the east in May 1942.

It suddenly struck me that this woman's life was like a weighty accusation. Or at least a severe reproach, a silent reproach to the country that had so cruelly ravaged her life. A country that had caught up a very young woman in its toils and now disgorged onto this dirty platform a bemused old lady, lost among these sunburnt faces. For the first time in my life I believed that this reproach was directed at me as well, and that I, too, in ways it was hard to formulate, had a responsibility for this elderly, solitary existence, reduced to great deprivation, forgotten there in an antediluvian building, in a township carved up by railway tracks, on the edge of the empty steppes. After all that she had done, given, suffered for this country . . . The people who surrounded me on the train, packed close together, laden with crates of vegetables they were bringing back from their kitchen gardens, had placid faces, tinged with routine, natural contentment. 'The simple contentment she has never had,' I thought, observing them. Not some copybook bliss, just a simple, contented, daily routine, a family life, in the pleasant and predictable round of the small facts of existence.

It was from that evening onwards that I would embark on reinventing her life, as if, by dreaming it differently, I could expiate the wrong my country had done her. The habit we had at the orphanage of remaking the life stories of our disgraced fathers would stand me in good stead. It would have taken little for her husband not to have been shot (how many times had I heard tales of condemned men saved by a miracle during the Stalin era), for them to have had children, for her to be living not in that old, dark house but over there, for example: I looked across at a handsome façade with balconies surrounded by pretty mouldings. She would have been reading books not to the young barbarian I was but to a refined and sensitive child, to her grandson and her granddaughter too, perhaps, two children who would have listened to her wide-eyed.

Reality often swept these daydreams away. But I set great store by them, telling myself that at least in this renascent life I could give Alexandra back her real Christian name. And her language, too, which sometimes, when she was speaking to me in French, lost a word or an expression, for which she would desperately rack her brains, with a mild look of distress in her eyes. This was not a case, I sensed, of banal forgetfulness or a failing in her ageing memory. No, this was an absolute loss, the disappearance of a whole world, her native land, which was being obliterated, word by word, in the depths of the snow-covered steppes where she had no one to talk to in her own language.

# Seven

When I arrived in Jacques Dorme's native town I felt no disorientation. In Paris I had lived in the rue Myrha, which cuts across the African bustle of the Boulevard Barbès. I had also lodged in the suburbs at Aubervilliers, later on in the outskirts of Montreuil, and subsequently in the Belleville district, where I had ended up no longer noticing the strangeness of this new country.

This little town in northern France was very much a part of that country.

The town hall, in a neat and tidy square, was reminiscent of those elderly Parisian ladies I used to pass occasionally near the Boulevard Barbès: survivors from another era, with carefully groomed clothes and hair, trotting along intrepidly amid this human cocktail from pulverized continents . . .

The safe island on which the town hall stood was indeed much reduced. The main street, elegant at the start, rapidly ran out of steam, disintegrated into rough façades, their windows filled in with breeze blocks. The window of a confectioner's was fractured in a number of places and patched with plywood. A little notice announced: 'Closed due to being fed up.' I consulted my street map, turned left.

On the telephone Jacques Dorme's brother had advised me to take a taxi from the station: 'It's quite a long way. We're at the edge of the town . . .' But I needed to walk, to see this town, to sense what it must have been like half a century earlier. I could not reconcile myself to the idea of climbing out of a taxi, ringing the front doorbell and going in like someone who knew the area.

A motor scooter passed at full speed, brushed against me, swerved in and out of overturned dustbins. A beer bottle rolled under my feet, I was not sure if it had been aimed at me or not. The sign bearing the street name was daubed with red. It took me a moment to decipher it: rue Henri Barbusse. Beneath a broken window, dangling from a rotary clothes dryer, scraps of cloth blew back and forth. The glass had been replaced by a blue plastic bag, an unexpected patch of colour on a grey-brown wall. Another window on the ground floor looked almost bizarre with its little vase of flowers and neat, pale curtains. And in the wan December air an aged hand was closing the shutters, a wrinkled face and the gleam of white hair, eyes that met mine: a woman who might have lived here at the time of Jacques Dorme.

The town soon flattened out beneath the roofs of empty warehouses and abandoned garages, disintegrated into moribund little bungalows. Modern residential buildings now made their appearance, having waited for the town to lose heart before thrusting up their towers, interspersed with four- or five-storey blocks of flats. I was subconsciously comparing them with the suburbs of Moscow, finding the dwellings here much better designed and with a more humane architecture, when at that moment I noticed a burned-out front entrance like the mouth of an enormous furnace, and a line of mailboxes thrown down on a patch of grass covered in rubbish sacks. The people I saw seemed in a hurry to get home and avoided me when I tried to stop them and ask the way. Two women, one of them very old, her face marked with blue ink, the other young and veiled, listened to me, staring at me in perplexity, as if the place I was looking for were the subject of some kind of taboo. The young woman pointed me in the right direction with a vague gesture and I saw her look back at me, still with that incredulous air.

The low-rise housing zone was separated from the new buildings by the Avenue de l'Egalité, which ran along beside a blackish, porous wall. I only realized there was a cemetery here when I reached the entrance. One of the gates had been ripped off and hung from the upper hinge. I went in without really going in, just glancing at the first of the graves. 'The Verdun sector', it said on a little pillar. The crosses took the form of swords: all of them too rusty for one to be able to read the names, some of them broken, lying there amid broken bottles, old newspapers, dog turds. Outside a car drove past, blaring out rhythmic chanting, a singer's cries of protest. The silence returned, mellowed by the rustling of bare branches in the wind.

As I was following the cemetery wall, and about to turn down into the residential streets, I saw this other car. A car surrounded by five or six youths, or rather cornered by them at a road junction. It was not, properly speaking, an assault. They were kicking the sides of the car, laughing and climbing onto the bonnet, tugging at the door handles. The driver, who was trying to get out to push them away, was forced to remain stooped, neither sitting nor standing, for they had trapped his leg in the door. One of them, a can of beer in his hand, was gargling and spitting out the froth into the car.

It may have been this spitting that propelled me towards

the group. I noticed the driver's foot, a fine black shoe, a long sock and the very pale skin revealed beneath the trouser leg which the edge of the door had rolled back, an old man's skin, criss-crossed by dark veins. There was nothing heroic about my impulse, just a sudden inability to tolerate the sight of this old foot, comically pawing the asphalt. And probably the outcome of my intervention would have been quite different had it not been for two motor scooters that suddenly emerged round the cemetery wall and began pursuing one another in and out of the narrow alleyways. Four of the young men clinging to the car ran off to watch the chase. The other two remained, finding that harassing the driver was more entertaining.

One of them continued spitting and choking with laughter. The other was leaning against the door with all his weight and drumming on the car roof with his fists, as on a tom-tom . . . I hit the spitting youth as hard as I could, with a blow designed to knock him down. He staggered, his back splayed against the car, and I had time to see a flash of surprise in his eyes, the astonishment of one who had thought himself unassailable. He dodged the second blow and began running, shouting that he would come back with his 'brothers'. I grasped the other one, in an attempt to free the door. He twisted round, spewing out a mouthful of the French I most detested: that new French, made up of verbal filth and acclaimed as the language of the young. The old man's leg was still trapped by the door. I saw a hand feverishly trying to wind up the window and on the passenger seat the figure of a woman, with very delicate fingers folded over a box of pastries. For several seconds the set-to seemed, as ever, ugly and long drawn out. As ugly as this young face was handsome ('a handsome face combined with a foul mouth,' I was to think later.) As long drawn out as the manoeuvring of the young man, unable to pull a flick-knife out of his pocket. He pressed the button too soon and the blade at once cut through the cloth of his jeans. I leaned my arm harder against his throat. His voice hissed, then fell silent. For a moment his mouth opened dumbly, then suddenly his eyes grew cloudy and at all once flickered in a basic animal refusal to suffocate. His body collapsed like that of a puppet. I loosened my grip, pushed him towards the pavement. He staggered away, stumbling, rubbing his throat and hissing threats in his broken voice.

The door slammed, the car drove off and turned into an avenue.

Now several minutes spent wandering about with a feeling of nausea, compounded of useless anger and belated fear, fear arriving in sickening gusts that corresponded to the buzzing of the scooters in the streets. But, most of all, a vivid awareness of the total futility of my intervention. I could at this very moment have been lying in the gutter with a flick-knife between my ribs. And it would have changed nothing and surprised no one, for there are so many small towns like this, so many old men attacked. Now my anger turns against the driver, who had had the stupidity to stop and parley instead of putting his foot down and driving home. I feel more remote than ever from this country. What am I doing interfering in its life, reprimanding young armed gorillas, playing the good citizen, with my stateless person's identity card in my pocket . . . ?

The burning sensation from these words delays my search. I finally find the Allée de la Marne but number sixteen appears to be non-existent. I cross the road twice, study each of the houses, certain that, without being able to see the number, I have recognized Jacques Dorme's. But the number, precisely, is missing. I walk along the street in the other direction: a sequence of two-storey houses, with bare gardens. In the depths of a room, a feeling of expectation, that goes back a long way. An open garage door and on the other side of the street, at number eleven, an old woman thrusting her hand into the mailbox, finding nothing, taking advantage of these moments to observe me. Or rather, she pretends to look for letters while scrutinizing this strange passer-by who is retracing his footsteps. So as not to alarm her I call out from some way off: 'Number sixteen, Madame?' Her voice is strangely beautiful, strong, an elderly singer's voice one might think: 'Why, it's over there, Monsieur. Just behind you . . .' I turn, take a few steps. The open garage door hides the ceramic circle with the number on it. Inside a man is cleaning the windscreen of his car with a sponge. I recognize him immediately: the old man with elegant black shoes. Jacques Dorme's brother, 'Captain', as I called him, in accordance with Alexandra's stories.

I tell him my name, remind him of our conversations on the telephone, my letters. His smile does not entirely succeed in obliterating the hint of sourness lurking in his wrinkles. I do not know if he recognizes me as the man who intervened just now. It seems as if he does not. He closes the garage, invites me to come up into the house, and on the front steps asks me this question, which ought to be utterly banal. 'Did you find it easily? Did you come by taxi?' It is not banal, a tiny quaver in his voice betrays the secret tension with which these words are uttered. So he has recognized me . . . Settled in the drawing-room, we talk about the town and succeed in avoiding the slightest allusion to what has just happened in the Avenue de l'Egalité. His wife enters, offers me her hand, those fragile fingers I saw clutching a beribboned cardboard box. Her face, with its Asiatic impassivity (she is Vietnamese), shows no trace of emotion. 'I'll bring tea,' she says with a slight smile and leaves us alone.

I have nothing new to tell him. In my first letter, thirty pages long, I set down with the assiduity of a chronicler everything I knew about Jacques Dorme, about Alsib, about the week the pilot spent in Stalingrad. No, not everything, far from that. Like an archaeologist, I simply wanted this history to be added to the history of their country, like a national art object discovered abroad and repatriated. I talk about my journey to Siberia, to the house on the Edge, about the Trident mountain . . . That journey, made at the beginning of the year (we are now in December), is still vividly present, with the sounds of the wind, voices made clear by the cold. However, my enthusiasm in recounting it seems to embarrass the Captain. He senses my purpose: the repatriation of a parcel of history that got lost in the snowy wastes of eastern Siberia. I feel his face growing tense, his eyes see me without seeing me, peering into a past that suddenly reappears in front of us in this drawing-room, on this December afternoon. I interpret his emotion incorrectly and lay my cards on the table: I am writing a book that will rescue the French pilot from oblivion, the press will be interested in him and, as I know the place where he died, it will be possible to bring his mortal remains back to France, to the town of his birth . . .

I break off, seeing his lips painfully stretched, attempting an unsteady smile. His voice is pitched higher than before, almost shrill: 'To France? To the town of his birth? What for? To bury him in a cemetery that's become a rubbish dump? In this town where people don't dare to leave their homes any more? For him to listen to that racket?'

A car drives along the street; the torrent of chanting backed by a rhythmic drumbeat rips into the house. The noise of scooters cuts through the rap. The Captain says, or rather shouts, something, but I do not hear him. He realizes I have not heard him. I catch only the last few words: '. . . to be spat upon . . .'

Time stands still. I watch his face as swift shudders pass across it, and his chin trembles. He is an old man fighting off tears with all his strength. I remain motionless, mute, totally incapable of any gesture or word that might break the deadlock of grief confronting grief. The wretched Parisian critic, who will later refer to me as an immigrant, will be right: I shall never be French for I do not know what should be said in a situation like this. In Russian I know. In French I shall never know and, indeed, I should never want to know what to say . . . His eyes remain dry, they simply grow red.

With an abrupt tensing of his jaw he succeeds in gaining control of his face, which now looks hollow, as if after a long period of mourning. In a dull, jaded voice he chokes more than he says: 'No, no, there's no point . . . The press, speeches . . . Too late . . . And besides, you know Jacques was a very private person . . .' I see his lips twitching again. He gets up, turns towards the photos hanging on the wall. He needs to be unobserved for a few moments. I get up too, and stand behind him, listening to his commentary. In one of the photos the two of them are on the front steps of the house. Of this house. In this street. The tone of his remarks is still uneven, often sliding up into high registers it is painful to hear.

The chink of crockery can be heard from the kitchen. He grasps at the pretext: 'This tea of yours, Li En, is it ready?' His wife appears at that very moment, a tray with teacups on it in her hands, as if to say: 'I wanted to leave the two of you to talk, man to man. Don't you understand?' He does understand, helps her to set down the tray, stops her leaving, squeezes her shoulders: 'You stay with our guest. I'll see to the cake . . .' He goes into the kitchen. His wife, seeing me in front of the photos, picks up the thread of the interrupted commentary. 'That one, that's in Saigon . . .' A jetty, the pale side of a boat, her and him, dressed in white, young, their eyes blinking in the sunlight. 'This one's in Senegal. And that's in your country, at Odessa. Eisenstein's famous steps . . .' She talks to me about their travels, not as tourists do, but simply running through the various stages of their life.

'Li, I can't find the little cake slice!' She smiles at me, excuses herself, goes to join her husband in the kitchen. I walk round the armchairs, stop at the other end of the drawing-room. A portrait on the wall: a young man with a serious, open face, a bushy moustache and, in the corner of the photo, the date, 1913. The father.

This hour spent in the house where Jacques Dorme was born leaves me with an impression of imminent departure. Not that of my return to Paris, no. Rather the clear perception that what we say is being uttered for the last time and that, when we have finished our tea, we shall have to get up, take a last look at the photos in their frames, leave the place behind. We all three experience, and each of us can sense in the others, the beginning of a separation, a distancing, now arising between us and the house, one that is all the more painful because our hands can still touch the back of this old armchair and our eyes still meet the gaze of a portrait on the wall.

And yet their house, a true family house, is deeply permeated with the slow memory of the generations, with the human aura taken on by furniture and objects, linking lives from father to son, marking deaths, greeting the return of prodigal children. I feel exactly as if I have returned after a long absence, to discover what I had known in Alexandra's house. The room where she used to read to me seems, in my memory, to be adjacent to this drawing-room where we are drinking tea. The France I pictured through all those pages we once read is here in the gaze of these portraits, in the words I am now hearing. But this rediscovered house will become a dream once more.

Our conversation, in which I know there must be no further mention of Jacques Dorme, often teeters on the brink of this erasure. The Captain talks about the church I saw on my way here, a local curiosity. And then falls silent, embarrassed, recalling at the same moment as myself, no doubt, the old walls covered in graffiti, the dark corners behind the apse stained with urine. He shows me a book with a red and gold cover, the first he read as a child. He opens it with a smile, declaims the first part of a sentence, closes it abruptly: the din of the joy-riding in the street stops him speaking. For several seconds we do not move, exchanging embarrassed glances, waiting for the racket to cease. Amid the rhythmic yelling of the singer a rhyme can be heard: 'He's in clink – she's in mink.' The class struggle . . .

Going out onto the front steps, we pause for a moment in the half-light of the winter dusk, the Captain fingering a bunch of keys, myself trying to make out the bottom of the garden where the trees give the illusion of a veritable wood. Li En speaks in a perfectly level voice, without bitterness: 'In the old days you could feel quite remote in the copse there. But now, with that car park . . .' I take a few steps. Beyond the branches of the trees looms a flat, ugly supermarket building, surrounded by a stretch of asphalt, from which comes the metallic clatter of trolleys being stacked. 'Right. We can leave now,' announces the Captain, and leans forwards to kiss Li En.

This simple remark, this word, 'leave', suddenly explains everything. We are not leaving, it is the country, their country, their France, that is moving away, being replaced by another country. This house, surrounded by bare trees and dark-green, almost black yew foliage, is evocative of the last rock of a submerged archipelago.

I shake hands with Li En, prepare to take my leave of the Captain, but he stops me: 'No, no, I'll drive you to the station,' and leads me towards the gate, despite my protestations. I sense that for him this is more than a gesture of courtesy. He needs to demonstrate to the foreigner I am that he is still at home in this street, this country.

As he is opening the garage I have time to take one more look at the front of the house, the gate with its railings, the steps up to the door. I tell myself that during the century now drawing to a close this house has twice witnessed the same scene: a man carrying a military knapsack on his shoulder walks over the road, reaches the crossroads and turns back to wave to a woman standing beside the gate at number sixteen. A man going off to the front. The crossroads . . . Where an hour ago the Captain's car was covered in spittle. In the darkness I see the beams of headlamps sweeping over the crossroads, engines roaring. The fun's not over yet.

The Captain invites me to get in, the car heads for the crossroads. He could turn off before he reaches it, go down one of the side roads. But we travel back past the precise place where the couple were set upon. A motor scooter appears, follows us, presses up close beside the car for several yards, then lets us go. I watch the Captain's face discreetly. It is a mask with tensed lips, his eyes slightly screwed up as if profoundly weary from seeing.

Just before we get there I try my luck one more time. I ask him if he would agree to his brother's story appearing under the cover of a fictitious name, that of a character in a novel. He seems to hesitate, then confides to me: 'You know, when he was very young all Jacques ever dreamed of was becoming a pilot. He had one idol, an ace in the Great War, René Dorme. He talked about him so often that we ended up nicknaming him "Dorme". We used to tease him: "Frère Jacques, dormez vous?" His friends at school always called him "Dorme". And he was proud of it, really. The few letters he sent from the front, he always signed them with that nickname . . .'

In the train I shall muster a review beneath my eyelids of the various stages in the life of this French pilot: Spain, Flanders, Poland, the Ukraine, Stalingrad, Alsib . . . Little by little, as the eyes slowly adjust to it, this life will take on the name of Jacques Dorme.

In the letter I received two years after our meeting the Captain made a few sober and appropriate remarks about the book I had sent him, the novel in which I told the story of Alexandra's life, or rather daydreamed about her life. Jacques Dorme did not appear in it. The Captain had no doubt taken this omission to be out of respect for our agreement. I had not had the courage to tell him the French pilot had been sacrificed because he was considered to be 'too true for a novel'. Like the old general in the middle of the sun-baked steppes beside the Volga . . .

His letter was penned in that precise and subtle French whose use was becoming rare in France. Struck by the elegance of his style, I did not immediately discern a slight hint of disappointment lurking behind his words: unspoken approval at seeing our agreement respected and at the same time this barely perceptible regret at not seeing it broken. Indeed, expressed in the lines he had written, or rather between these lines, was a hope that by means of some literary magic Jacques Dorme might live again, without, as it were, being subjected to the idle curiosity of a country he would no longer have recognized as his own.

It was the contradiction I had sensed in his letter, this hesitation between a fear of complete oblivion and a refusal to condone a revelatory memoir, that suggested this unpretentious genre to me: a chronicle in which the ruling device would be faithfulness to the bare framework of the facts. With the pilot's name replaced by his nickname.

A year later my thoughts turned again to this modest narrative task on a journey back from Berlin. In no other city had I seen so many efforts to commemorate the past and such a triumphal will to flatten this past beneath the foundations of a phoenix-like capital. If the truth be told, I preferred this brutal flattening to what was being thought and said in France. To the condescending irony of the historian I once found myself sitting next to on a television panel. With his petty air of mocking disdain, he had spoken of 'Adolf Hitler's pygmy campaigns'. The participants had smiled, as if at an epigram, before continuing with the verbal ping-pong, noting France's shameful inaction and the fact that the severity of the Russian winter had happily blocked the Nazis' advance . . . I should have made an instant riposte, reminded them that this particular pygmy warrior had defeated the most powerful armies in the world and, having come close to the carotid artery of the Volga, had come within an ace of final victory. Impossible to get a word in, the talk came thick and fast. Then the memory of a gesture came back to me: a French pilot spreads out a map and covers the violet hexagon of his country with a matchbox, which he then applies to the red expanse of the Soviet Union. This gesture would have been the best possible response to these television strategists. But the broadcast was already reaching its conclusion with a sneering observation by one of the participants: 'What happened at Stalingrad was that one brand of totalitarianism wrung another one's neck. That's all!'

At this moment I felt able to understand the Captain's hesitations better than ever . . . Even as our make-up was being removed four or five young women were waiting their turn to be powdered for the cameras, all in a morbidly excited state as guests in the antechambers to these media bazaars often are. They were novelists and the theme they were due to discuss was: 'Sex: can the pen have the last word?'

After the broadcast that evening, I re-read an old pamphlet I had found among the bookstalls beside the Seine. Printed on terrible, dull, rough paper, it had been published barely three months after the fall of France in June 1940 and, drawing no historical lessons, brought together the military exploits of the French campaign. A fragmentary chronicle and, of course, one subject to German censorship, a series of sketches made at the time: the defence of a village, hand-to-hand fighting in a township, the loss of a ship . . . Dates. Names. Ranks. A war seen by soldiers and not the one acted out all over again in the history books half a century later:

Following this, a retreat over seven days of continuous fighting brought the regiment into the Charmes region. Four French divisions, drawn up in defence and surrounded on all sides, fought there without hope. The Eighteenth Infantry Regiment had lost more than half its strength . . .

The battle then took on a character of extraordinary ferocity. They fought with grenades and at certain points with bayonets. Captain Cafarel defended his own command post himself, and was killed . . . During these two days the Second Battalion of the

Seventeenth Regiment of the Algerian Infantry Corps lost twelve out of its fifteen officers, all but four of its NCOs, four-fifths of its strength. They died heroically, without having yielded an inch . . .

The strength of the Division was now reduced to a few men. At 1800 hours, seeking to complete the operation, the enemy launched a massed attack. Using the weapons of the wounded and dead, the cavalry of the Second Division resisted. The machine guns fired their last rounds. The enemy was repelled . . .

The torpedo boat *Foudroyant* sank rapidly. For a few minutes the ship's stern stayed above the water. With magnificent gallantry, Commander Fontaine remained standing upon the stern until his vessel had sunk entirely from view . . .

That night the chronicle of Jacques Dorme's life truly began to write itself inside me. I knew that, in addition, I should have to talk about that boy who was to discover a country where the four gentlemen of Aquitaine lived, as well as the soldier in the last square and that other one, who died on the banks of the Meuse 'almost as destitute of money as when he had come from thence to Paris'. Thirty years on they all had a close kinship in my mind with Captain Cafarel, Commander Fontaine and the Second Battalion of the Seventeenth Algerian Infantry Corps.

I went back to Jacques Dorme's town a week after my return from Berlin. My plan on this occasion was to stay in a hotel and spend several days there, so as to have time to reconstruct the town as it used to be, in the way one restores a mosaic; but one in which, instead of tesserae, there would be the hundred-year-old tree beside that church covered in graffiti, the sign for a bakery, the florid lettering that had not changed since the years between the wars; the picture of a street untouched by the ugliness of satellite dishes. I thought I should be able, if only for the space of a glance, to reconstruct what Jacques Dorme saw in his youth, what his native town, his native land had been.

I telephoned the Captain several times without ever hearing either his voice or that of Li En. Silent, too, was the familiar refrain of their answering machine, with its ironic politeness, which had always made me smile. If I had had to invent such moments in the plot of a novel, I should probably have spoken of growing unease, imagining the worst . . . In reality my first thought was simply of death. And the most intense response provoked by this thought was not sadness, nor even remorse at having delayed and wasted time on all those trivialities that generally go with a book's publication. No, I felt afflicted with mutism. It was as if the language in which I had spoken with the Captain were no longer spoken by anyone else.

In the train I told myself that this feeling of speaking a dead language was one that Alexandra must have experienced throughout her life in Russia.

In the Allée de la Marne there were no signs of death. There was simply a sense of absence, emptiness behind the closed shutters of number sixteen. The garage door was covered in fluorescent scrawls that had lost their aggressiveness with the passage of time. The lengths of wire fastening the 'For Sale' sign to the gate were rusty. But there were no papers spilling out of the mailbox. I turned round on hearing the voice I recognized: it was the neighbour from number eleven, whom I had supposed to be a retired professional singer. 'I'm the one who collects all the junk mail. You have to do that, otherwise they set fire to it. That's what they did to my neighbour across the road . . .' She opened the box, took out a leaflet. She had spoken of 'them' without any rancour, with resignation, rather, the way they talk about the weather in those Northern lands.

'Li En has gone to Canada. She's thinking of settling over there, near her sister . . .' We walked diagonally across the road, from number sixteen to number eleven. Thinking I was in the know, the 'singer' did not say much more, just a few words about Li En going away, taking her husband's ashes.

Left alone in the Allée de la Marne, I pictured those last moments before her departure very intensely. Li En's face, that pale, impassive mask and the force of the Asian stare that spoke of her pain better than a face distorted with grief would have done. I saw her walking down the steps, closing the gate, taking the steering wheel . . .

At the crossroads she had passed over I stopped. In the opaque humidity of the dusk the streetlamps were becoming suffused with a milky blue. In a telephone box with broken doors a receiver dangled, and there was a sound of whispering voices, just as if someone could still be making a call there. The wind ruffled the charred pages of a telephone directory.

At the centre of the row of houses beside the Allée de la Marne I could just make out the gate of number sixteen. I reflected that to understand Jacques Dorme's country those hundred yards were enough, the distance between the house a man has just walked out of to go to the war and this crossroads, where he turns back to take a last look at those who will remain behind to wait for him.

. . . As it takes off the helicopter banks steeply and I have time to glimpse the house on the Edge, the glow from the kitchen windows. It seems to me as if the pilot is also glancing at this radiance. Perhaps the very last glimmer of light between here and the Arctic Ocean, I say to myself, and I find it difficult to get the measure of this white infinity opening up before us and ingesting our frail cockpit, like a bubble of warm air, in a huge, icy inhalation.

The untouched emptiness of the Chersky mountain range.

The height of the peaks is increasing imperceptibly, as can be judged from the disappearance of the little dark stripes, the trunks of the dwarf trees that until a few moments ago were still managing to find a foothold at this extreme limit of the tundra. Higher up there are only two textures, ice and rock. And two kinds of surface: the granite hard snowfields and the naked crags of the pinnacles.

It was on one of these snowfields that we landed, after an hour of flight. Seen from above, the ground appeared quite vast but as we descended it became enclosed between two white walls, revealing itself to be a long hanging valley flanked by steep, icy slopes. I help the two Levs to unload their equipment and balance it on a small, flat sledge.

'How many bangers have you got?' the pilot asks them. Big Lev gets muddled up trying to count them. Little Lev calls out with the zealous air of a boy scout: 'Twelve, chief. We'll start when the sun's up and we'll be finished before it sets. After that, just time to get back on board.' The sun has not yet risen. Today it will be there for an hour and thirty-five minutes, the pilot explains to me . . . The geologists move off in the direction of a slope that rises in uneven terraces. Extending his arm towards a rocky defile, the pilot shows me the way. I shall have to skirt the obstacle of a glacier, leave the valley, traverse a narrow saddle until the moment when the summit, which will at first look like a vast monolith, divides up into three bare peaks: the Trident . . . 'They have twelve charges today, our trusty bomb-aimers. So you'll hear twelve explosions. Count them carefully. At the last one turn back immediately. They'll still have their rocks to gather up. Then we'll take off at once. We shan't be able to wait for you . . .'

I set off, glancing several times at the crenellation of the mountains all about our landing-ground, trying to take note of a few features. Already the sky is almost light, the sun will rise in half an hour . . . Just as I am making my way round a rock that has an icy fissure gouged out of it and am losing sight of the landing-ground, I hear the first explosion.

The echo of the seventh, multiplied by the mountain, reaches me at the very moment when a huge, rocky peak, of a silvery density, comes into view. Its shape is sugges-tive of a great milky flint, coarsely sculpted by the winds. I consult my watch. The sun has already been up for twenty minutes. 'Been up' means it slips onto the level of

181

the horizon, invisible behind the peaks, before disappearing for a night more than twenty hours in duration.

As with all mountains, the summit seems to recede as one draws closer. My progress is engulfed in a time that pushes me back and slows me down, like the hard snow on which I slither about. The eighth explosion is followed almost immediately by the ninth, just as if it were its echo. And the summit is still monolithic in form. Perhaps, after all, it is not the Trident. I look about me: there are three or four other peaks all towering up in much the same location.

The echo of the tenth explosion catches up with me, already a dull, matt sound, which gives a measure of the distance it has travelled. The sun, invisibly, has been in the sky for three-quarters of an hour. I lengthen my stride, try to run, fall. The snowy ground I push against to raise myself has the dry roughness of emery.

Suddenly narrow blades of light slice into the summit. Its surface, which seemed flat, moulds itself into facets, slopes, grooves, where deep violet shadows slumber. The sun has burst through some hidden crevice, an aperture that brings this brief luminous vision to life. The next explosive charge detonates a very long way off. The sequence of reverberations is longer than before. The eleventh? Or already the twelfth, the last one? I do not know any more if I have counted correctly. I remember the pilot's words: 'We shan't wait for you. Otherwise I'll be hacking all this loose rock to pieces in the dark with my propeller.' I begin to run, my eyes on the summit, slip several times, the ground is no longer firm, the wind drives long ribbons of spindrift before it. At every step, however, the change is perceptible. The rays of light grow broader, break up the summit, dividing the mountain into three immense crystals. This looks less like a trident than a bird's broken wing. I stumble into a slope, stop, my breathing flayed raw by the cold. The greyish mass of a glacier bars the way. I study the three illuminated sections of the mountain: the rock is barely whitened with frost, the snow, rare in these lands with their dry winters, fails to cling to the smooth walls. Vertical buttresses, ravines, high cols where frozen snow accumulates, scarcely re-shaped by the millennia. And the rays of light already beginning to fade. Nothing else. Nothing . . .

Suddenly I see the cross formed by the aircraft.

Two dark crossed lines against the pale suede of the hoar-frost. They are not in the triangles of sunlight on the summit but much lower down, near the base of the massif. The silhouette of the aircraft is easily recognizable, it is not a plane that has broken up in a crash, but, in attempting to land, it has become embedded in the rock and has remained there, welded to this mountain, to this arctic wasteland, its nights without end.

No thought speaks within me. No emotion. Not even joy at having achieved the goal. Only the certainty of experiencing the essence of what I had to understand.

The sun's breakthrough is weaker now. But the aircraft is still visible. I can even see the gleam of the cockpit. Beneath its glass a glimmer of life can be sensed. A silent life, focused on a past, of which soon nothing more will remain on this earth. The life that, clumsily, our words sometimes refer to as death, sometimes oblivion, some-times the memory of men.

Then the phrase uttered by that tall old man comes to

my mind, as he tried to speak of this life and the distance that separates us from it. '. . . They can look up to the Heavens without turning pale and upon the Earth without blushing.' In a past long dreamed of and suddenly present, a pilot leaps from his cockpit and stands beside the aircraft, one hand resting on the edge of a wing. I am infinitely close to his silence, I sense the focus of the gaze he directs at the Earth. An old wooden house, lost in the midst of the steppes, a night of war, a woman's slow words, the first ripples of a summer storm, a brief love, whose infinite duration trickles away in a cascade of beads from a broken necklace . . .

The reverberation from the explosion is a long one and from its echoes arises a prolonged, billowing vibration that becomes increasingly limpid. A resonance that goes on refining itself until it seems to be ringing out beyond our lives, in a distant place, of which this arctic day is but an ephemeral reflection. Here the echo's notes are fading away, obliterated beneath the hiss of the frost needles that the wind sweeps across the ground. But over there the man standing beside his aircraft hears them still. A long farewell song, a song of light.

The ray of sunlight has been gone for a moment now, the cross of the aircraft fades in the swiftly advancing pallor of the night. Snow squalls start to blur the outline of the mountains. I shall not be able to see the rock outcrops noted as waymarks on my outward journey. Yet the vibration of the last echo still seems to survive among the summits. A subtle resonance that resists the wind. I sense its vibrations deep within me.

All I have to do to find my way back is not cease hearing it.